THE EVIDENCE YOU WILL HEAR

THE
EVIDENCE
YOU
WILL
HEAR

Hamilton Jobson

PERENNIAL LIBRARY

Harper & Row, Publishers, New York
Cambridge, Philadelphia, San Francisco, Washington
London, Mexico City, São Paulo, Singapore, Sydney

A hardcover edition of this book was originally published by Charles Scribner's Sons in 1975. It is here reprinted by arrangement with Charles Scribner's Sons.

First PERENNIAL LIBRARY edition published 1986.

Library of Congress Cataloging-in-Publication Data

Jobson, Hamilton.
    The evidence you will hear.

    I. Title.
[PR6060.022E9   1986]   823'.914   86–45120
ISBN 0–06–080821–7 (pbk.)

086 87 88 89 90 OPM 10 9 8 7 6 5 4 3 2 1

THE EVIDENCE YOU WILL HEAR

CHAPTER 1

The five-forty-five slid into the station, groaned to a halt and disgorged its tired commuters who scurried like ants along the platform, converged on the ticket collector and then fanned out again, just as they did every evening of the week from Monday to Friday.

Among them, Joe Murray and Tom Purdy walked side by side, briefcases under arms, umbrellas clicking steel tips on the footpath. They turned along the tree-lined Beech Avenue and Purdy, who had been doing most of the talking, was moved to protest as he lagged behind. "What's all the hurry? You seem to forget that your legs are twice as long as mine."

Murray laughed and shortened his stride. "Sorry."

"Something's urging you on," said Purdy, "and . . ." He squinted into the distance and forgot what he was going to say. "Isn't that a police car near your house?"

"I think it is. Probably for next door; they had a burglary last month."

They slowed down and Purdy lifted the latch of his gate. "See you in the morning?"

1

"As usual. Should've finished your book by then. I'll bring it with me."

"No hurry."

A brief wave from both of them and Murray was off the leash. Something *was* urging him on and he couldn't get home soon enough. He had been with the same firm of accountants for fourteen years and had known for some time that a partnership was in the offing. They didn't want to lose him. Today it had come through and the first to hear about it had to be Joyce. Earlier he had tried to ring her.

It was a grey police car. The metallic sound of a radio conversation filtered through the open window and the driver, on his own, sat with his head down, reading a small blue book. Murray gave the car a final glance and felt for his door key as he went up his front path. He was in the hall before he heard the voices, first his wife's in a tone which caused him to frown and then a man's, deep and with a Scottish accent.

Leaving his umbrella and briefcase in the hall, he pushed open the sitting-room door and it was the expression on his wife's face rather than the presence of the police sergeant perched on the edge of an easy chair which caused his frown to deepen. He was a large policeman with bulky shoulders and a huge bottom which covered the width of the chair. His flat cap rested on one knee and his round, florid face showed a guarded concern. They looked up at Murray and the policeman lurched to his feet. "Good evening, sir."

"What's happened?" said Murray, glancing from one to the other.

His wife's lips trembled and the policeman said: "It's your daughter, sir. She hasn't come home. You *are* Mr. Murray?"

"Yes, but..." Murray looked at his wife. "I don't understand. You always pick her up in the car."

She covered her face with her hands. "I went to sleep," she said in a tearful, muffled voice. "It's terrible. I went to sleep."

The sergeant spoke sympathetically. "I have told her, sir, that this sort of thing often happens. We get it all the time

2

with children. Only last week we found one, after an eight-hour search, hiding under the bedclothes."

"Did you?" said Murray. "Well, my daughter doesn't hide under bedclothes. She doesn't hide anywhere. There must be something wrong." He turned his watch arm. "Why, it's well over two hours! What've you done?"

"All we can at the moment. We've called at the houses of several of her friends and searched the school and the parks and also a couple of buildings. As far as we can make out, a lady across the road saw her last, walking along the Boreham Road towards home."

"When was that?"

"About quarter to four. She asked her if she wanted a lift but the girl refused, saying that her mother was coming for her."

Murray, ashamed of his moment of panic, went over to his wife and put his arm around her. "It's probably as the officer says. We mustn't get stewed up unnecessarily now. Maybe she's gone into a friend's house, someone we don't know about. They don't always think, and after all she is only a child."

"She wouldn't. I know she wouldn't."

"Well, sir," said the sergeant, "I just came back in case she'd turned up, and for any other information your wife could give me. We've got her description and a photograph and we'll keep looking." He went to the door. "I'd better be on my way."

"Yes. Yes, of course," said Murray, "and thanks."

He sank on to a chair, stifling the dreadful thoughts which passed through his mind until he had a grip on himself. Over the past six months, three child murders in Coolidge, and Coolidge wasn't all that far away! They hadn't caught anybody yet. God, no! He mustn't think on these lines. But Joyce would, and she would never forgive herself. He heard her say between sobs: "I haven't got you anything to eat," and he was torn between worry and compassion.

"Never mind about that," he said, "I had too much for

lunch anyway. Tell me, dear, what time did you go to get her?"

"At ten to four. I woke up suddenly and saw the clock."

"Did you look for her on the way?"

She nodded. "Most of them had gone when I got there. I went into the school and saw the caretaker, and I went up and down the road, and then I didn't know what to do."

"I can't understand it. It's a main road but, as you say, she's not the sort to go wandering off. She *must* have gone in somewhere. Look, this going to sleep, there's nothing in that. A lot of children walk home alone anyway. She's had to do it sometimes."

"There's another thing. She's watching a serial on television. It comes on at five and she never misses it."

"That's it, then. She's gone in somewhere to look at it and forgotten the time."

"I can't believe that. *We* wouldn't have another child in here like that, would we, not without making sure the parents knew?"

"It's no use speculating. Let's do something. We'll ask Stella if one of them can come in just in case Angela arrives home, and we'll look everywhere."

She nodded dully and when, an hour later, they returned and a moment's hopeful eagerness was dashed by a shake of their neighbour's head, she seemed to crumple, but there were no tears.

Men travel from far and wide to join a police force, a practice which is encouraged by the authorities. Sergeant Bill Gisling was a native of Grantown-on-Spey and twenty of his forty-one years he had spent in the force, twelve as a constable and eight as a sergeant. He had struggled through his first promotion examination, which he knew was his limit, and despite his lack of future prospects had eventually been promoted.

He was a good practical policeman and, although the finer points of the law sometimes escaped him, he had ample com-

4

mon sense and his own forceful but effective way of dealing with tricky situations.

For one who could be so hard and tough when necessary, he had an unusually soft spot for children and whenever one was missing he worried beyond the call of duty. He knew that in ninety-nine per cent of these cases they turned up again, and he never conveyed his own concern to the parents, but until they were found it stayed with him, constantly on his mind.

When he left the Murrays', Gisling sat in the car looking at the coloured photograph and holding it so that the driver, Constable Jim Hough, could also see it. It was of a pretty, intelligent-looking child in a blue school blazer edged with gold, her long brown hair tied at the back with a gold ribbon.

"Fine-looking kid," said Hough. "Anything more to go on?"

Gisling slipped the photograph inside his pocket. "Not a thing. I think this is going to be serious. She's not the sort to get up to the usual tricks. I hope I'm wrong, by heck, I do, but I've got a feeling about it. Let's get back to the station and I'll have another word with the inspector."

Inspector John Murphy wasn't in a particularly good mood. Things hadn't gone too well for him lately and he had much on his mind. A process report which he had recommended for prosecution had backfired on him for lack of an essential piece of evidence which he had overlooked. Costs had been awarded against the police and the magistrate, a stipendiary who suffered from a troublesome gastric ulcer, had made some caustic comments. The superintendent who had appended his signature to the report was far from pleased. The fact that he hadn't looked into it too deeply himself had only aggravated the situation and increased his disapproval and resentment of the inspector's lapse.

As is so often the case when such things happen, other irritations become magnified, and the inspector was beginning to wish he hadn't given up smoking some six months previously. The missing girl hadn't caused him the same degree of concern as it had Sergeant Gisling but it was a disturbing incident in an already disturbing day.

The admin. sergeant knocked and came in. The inspector glared at the pile of papers deposited in his in-tray and grunted without looking up. When the sergeant had gone, he sifted through some of them and then let them fall back. The flat, square, electric clock on his desk, left there by his predecessor, showed that it was five past seven and he decided it was time for some light refreshment in the canteen. He was opening the door on his way out when Sergeant Gisling appeared.

"About the missing girl, sir, I'd like to see you."

"Hasn't she turned up?" said the inspector, going back to his desk.

"No, sir."

"Come in then and shut the door."

Gisling slowly and thoughtfully closed the door behind him. "I don't think she *will* turn up."

The inspector's eyebrows bounced up and down.

"It's now three hours," said Gisling. "We've searched all the likely places and I've seen a few people who know her, including the school teacher. Something's gone wrong."

"This would have to happen," said the inspector standing up abruptly, "on top of everything else!"

"I was thinking of the girl, sir."

"Are you being impertinent, Sergeant?"

"I don't think so, sir."

"Well, it sounded like it. I've got a girl of my own and I'm not without feeling. But you know what happens? We get everybody out, turn everywhere upside down and little Johnny has been hiding in the coal shed because he's got a bad report or he's pinched something."

"This is nothing like that."

"All right." The inspector sank wearily back on to his chair. "Give me the details."

"She left school at half past three with the others. Some of them were picked up by their parents and others walked, but she was outside after the others had gone."

"How d'you know that?"

"Her school teacher saw her and asked her if she was all right. The girl said she was waiting for her mother."

"How did you manage to see the teacher?"

"The head teacher was still there and he gave me her address. At about quarter to four a Mrs. Johnson, who lives near the Murrays, was driving down Boreham Road with her own children when she saw the girl walking towards home. She was then about a hundred yards from the school near the junction of Burlescombe Road. Mrs. Johnson stopped and asked her if she wanted a lift and again she said her mother was coming for her."

"You say that was at a quarter to four?"

"Within a few minutes, according to Mrs. Johnson, and she was quite definite about it. Mrs. Murray, who'd gone to sleep in the chair, arrived at the school at four, and she was definite about that. But there was no sign of the child."

"So she disappeared between quarter to four and four o'clock roughly?"

"Looks like it, sir. If she'd kept walking towards home, Mrs. Murray would have seen her. She said she was on the look-out all the way."

"What else makes you so pessimistic?"

"As I see it, she'd already refused a lift from a neighbour so it's unlikely she'd accept one from anyone else within fifteen minutes. The next junction after Burlescombe is Southborough Road. The next one past that is Kent Avenue, and I doubt if she would have reached that. The park and building sites are even farther on but we gave them a good going-over in case. As I said, I've spoken to her teacher and a few of the neighbours and some of her friends, and I'm convinced she's not the type of child to clear off on her own and in any case not for all this time."

Gisling took out the photograph and put it in front of the

inspector, who studied it for a while and then looked up, his face now serious and alert. "How many men have you on it?"

"Two car patrol crews, two pandas and me—that's even."

"Get them together and call at every house from the school to her home. Divide the road into sections and tell them I want a record of every call and who lives there."

"Right, sir. I'll leave the photograph with you, shall I?"

"Yes. I'll get on to Divisional HQ," said the inspector and dialled the number as the sergeant went out.

Joe Murray was in his garden, either walking about aimlessly or standing and staring at nothing in particular. What Sergeant Gisling suspected, he knew! His daughter would not willingly have been away for so long and the possibilities which came to him were too awful to contemplate. But he couldn't help contemplating them. He had heard of people ageing in minutes, their hair suddenly turning white, and now he could understand it.

Memories brought added torture to his already tortured mind: his wedding day over fourteen years ago; Joyce as she used to be, radiant, vivacious, full of enthusiasm; her two miscarriages and the gradual change to introspection and an almost pathological lack of self-confidence. He had wondered at times if he had been partly to blame, if in his own unwavering good health and physical strength he had not always been as understanding and considerate as he might have been. But the slightly cowed, martyred air she had assumed had often annoyed him. They had begun to drift apart—although deep down he knew he would always love her. And then, when it seemed that they would have to resign themselves to a childless marriage, Angela had come and it had all changed back again.

He heard the rattle of the gate latch and looked up sharply. But it was Purdy who was walking across the lawn towards him, his normally cheerful face straight and serious. "Joe!" I've just heard about Angela. Is it true?"

"It's true."

"I rang at the front door but couldn't get any answer. Where's Joyce?"

"Indoors. I can't do anything with her. Stella has been in and she's coming back later."

"Hell, Joe, can't we do something?"

"What *can* we do now? I've been everywhere I can think of and the police are still looking."

"I'm going to rustle up some help. You're needed here with Joyce if she's as you say."

"The police are doing all they can."

"I expect they are but it won't do any harm. I'll get Bristow and Stringer up the road and between us we can ring round. Go through the cricket club for a start."

"It's good of you. It'll be dark soon enough."

"Not properly for another two hours. I'll get moving!"

Murray nodded as if he only half understood but when Purdy had reached the gate he called out: "Thanks, Tom."

Harry Bristow carried the last of his cases downstairs and put it with the others in the hall. Now it had finally come, it was a funny feeling. But it was inevitable. They had both known it for months. His wife stood just inside the doorway, as calm as if he were the gas man on his way out. The tears, the railing, the insults and recriminations had all been used up until they were meaningless.

He ran a finger between his collar and his thick bull neck. "I'll want to see the kids regularly. You understand that?"

She nodded and they stood in silence.

"I'll load up," he said but as he picked up the heaviest case the telephone rang. She answered it and then held out the handset to him. "It's for you."

He took it and uncoiled the flex before he put it to his ear. "Hallo! Bristow here."

"Hallo, Harry; Tom Purdy. We need your help. Now, listen. Joe Murray's daughter, she's missing. Left school at half past three and hasn't come home. I'm not going into details but it's serious."

Bristow turned his head and stared at his wife as he listened and, noting the expression on his face, her manner changed.

"...the point is, we're organizing a search party to supplement the police. Can you join in?"

"Christ, yes!" said Bristow.

"All right. We're meeting in ten minutes at the junction of Boreham Road and Beech Avenue."

"I'll be there."

"What is it?" said his wife as he put the phone down.

"Joe Murray's kid, she's missing, and they think something's happened to her."

"What? Angela?"

"Yes. I'm going to join a search party."

"I'll take your cases back upstairs," she said.

Other telephones were ringing. George Stringer, who had just fallen off a pair of steps and was rubbing a bony knee, limped down the hall and lifted the receiver. "Joe's kid's missing? Sure I'll be along. Wife's got the car but I've my old bike in the shed. I'll pump up the tyres and join someone else when I get there."

Sergeant Gisling, who was with his men on the house-to-house enquiry, saw the cars assembling in the distance and decided to investigate. He had nearly reached them when Stringer, pedalling like mad on his creaking bicycle, swept past him and nearly fell off when he tried to stop and his brakes failed.

The group round one of the cars saw the sergeant coming and the hubbub and voices quietened as they looked at him expectantly. "Any news of her?" one of them asked.

Gisling realized then. "No," he said. "We're calling at every house in the road. What's going on here?"

Purdy detached himself. "We're all friends of Joe Murray and we're making up a search party before it gets too dark. Any suggestions?"

"That's good of you. We've been through the park and the

10

two building sites and the school. I reckon you could divide up into four groups and do each side of the town. There are a couple of quarries and some farmland." Gisling glanced at his watch. "Better get moving if you're going to do any good."

He was buttonholed as he moved off. "D'you reckon it's the same bastard? D'you think it is?"

"I don't know, sir. I don't like to think about it. Let's try and find her first."

Farther along the road Gisling pressed the button of his personal radio. It would be advisable to keep the inspector in the picture.

Stringer had teamed up with Purdy and dusk was setting in when they reached the east quarry, a huge white hole in the ground spotted with straggling bushes and patches of grass. Purdy let the car run down the hard road to the bottom and the ratchet clicked as he pulled up his handbrake.

"Nothing over that side," he said, surveying the bare, uneven surface. "Let's stroll over and look round these bushes on the other side."

They got out and followed a path made by tyre tracks which wound round potholes and loose scrub.

"Someone's been along here in a car recently," said Stringer.

"So they may have. I've got more respect for my springs."

They were some hundred feet from a large clump of bushes when Purdy slowed his stride. "There's a car there," he said, "a green one. I can just see a bit sticking out."

Stringer moved to alter his view. "So there is."

They went on more cautiously and when they rounded the screen of foliage Stringer whispered: "Well, I'm buggered! It's *my* car."

They peered into the car and Purdy went cold. There was a movement of naked flesh and a woman's startled face stared at them from behind a man's shoulder. Purdy turned and followed Stringer who staggered away. They were half way back to his own car before Purdy said anything. "Hell, George! Say something for God's sake!"

"What is there to say?" said Stringer and was violently sick on the ground.

There was an awkward silence and when they got back to the car Stringer carried on past it. Purdy, who had opened his door, called after him. "George! Where are you going?" There was no response and he again shouted: "George!"

Stringer stopped and turned. "You go on. I'm going to walk back."

Purdy started the engine and drove after him. Then he slowed to a crawl and put his head out of the window. "Don't be a bloody fool, George. This is no time for you to be alone. Get in."

Stringer tramped doggedly on and called back: "It's just the time to be on my own. I want to think."

"It's about five miles."

"What does that matter? Leave me, Tom, please."

"I don't like it."

"Promise me one thing—don't tell anybody or drop any hints?"

"Of course I won't. What d'you think I am?"

"Go on, then. And thanks!"

Purdy stared at him for a few moments. "All right," he said. "But come and see us tomorrow. If there's anything I can do!"

Apathetically Stringer watched the car pull away and disappear in a cloud of dust as it turned on to the main road. For a while he moved like an automaton, dimly aware of police vehicles which passed him and groups of people he passed.

Gradually the questions forming in his mind demanded consideration. Why, for God's sake, why? There'd been no hint of it. She hadn't seemed over-sexed, a bit on the cool side if anything. Once a fortnight, sometimes once a week. They'd been married long enough—ten years! No kids. Perhaps that was it? But it couldn't be; she hadn't wanted them. Took the pill regularly.

And they got on all right. The occasional tiff but nothing

12

much. He tried to remember when it must have first started, her taking the car off on her own. "You don't mind, dear, do you? I want to call and see Helen." Sometimes it was Joan. "You'd be bored with woman's talk." Probably she had seen Helen, or Joan, but not for long.

Who was he? All he'd seen was a broad back and a mop of dark hair. And he'd heard him grunting.

He was still speculating when he reached his house. He opened the garage doors first. The car was inside.

She wasn't downstairs. He didn't go up for some time and when he did he saw that she was in bed, lying with her face covered by the sheet. He lifted his own pillow and collected his pyjamas. He was at the door again when she sat up. "What are you going to do?"

"Sleep in the other bedroom."

"I don't mean that. What are you going to do . . . about us?"

"I don't know. What are you going to do?"

"I don't know."

CHAPTER 2

Chief Superintendent Dekker surveyed himself in the hall mirror, adjusted his bow tie and gave his formidable grey moustache an admiring flick with the back of a finger. Then he glanced at his watch and went to the foot of the stairs. "Jenny! Aren't you ready yet?"

Her voice floated down. "Two minutes."

"For crying out loud! You said that half an hour ago." With an irritable shrug he went out to his car and was cleaning off a few bird specks from the windscreen when she appeared, lifting the long, tight-fitting evening dress as she stepped along the path. Perhaps it was worth it, he thought. She looks pretty good and it was a sheer waste of time complaining. He wondered what it would be that she would remember that she had forgotten this time when they were half way up the road.

"We've plenty of time," she said as she settled in beside him. "No one will be there before nine."

"It started at half past seven," he said and turned the ignition key.

"Blast! I've forgotten my wrap."

14

He leaned back and made a face. "What d'you want that for?"

"I must have it."

"All right. Where is it?"

"I left it on the bed."

He switched off and got out. "Is there anything else, because I'm not going back again?"

"Nothing else. At least I don't think so."

He raised his eyes to the heavens and went back indoors. As he was about to leave with the wrap over his arm, the telephone rang and his first inclination was to ignore it. Then he knew he couldn't. He was the officer in charge of the uniform branch of the whole division. Like most people, he had his shortcomings but he was a conscientious policeman and twenty-four-hour responsibility went automatically with higher authority.

It was the chief inspector from Divisional Headquarters. "Sorry to trouble you, sir, but I can't contact the superintendent. We've a child missing at Forebridge and I think it's serious."

"I see. What's the score?"

"A girl of nine—didn't come home from school. The chaps there have done all they can and I understand the neighbours have started a search on their own. The point is that there's nothing about this girl which gives much hope, and in view of the Coolidge business I couldn't leave it."

Dekker blew through his teeth and accepted the inevitable. "I'll be down. I'm glad you rang. You only just caught me; I was on my way out."

"Shall I start preparing, sir?"

"Yes. Get hold of the Chief Inspector, Traffic, and tell him we'll want full coverage and equipment: floodlights, mobile stations, canteen—and the dogs, don't forget them. Get some maps there too and tell Inspector Murphy at Forebridge to clear an office for the job and keep an extension open. I expect I'll be at least half an hour."

"Very good, sir. I'll get cracking."

15

The chief superintendent dropped the wrap on a chair and went out to his wife. "Good job you did forget something this time. A child's missing at Forebridge and I'm going down there. I shan't bother to change."

The small sub-station at Forebridge was a hive of activity when, still in his dinner suit, Dekker arrived. Two dog vans and a large emergency vehicle were lined up outside with three patrol cars. Three utility vehicles were parked in the yard at the back and the place was milling with policemen and civilians. Dekker took a brief look round and went in by the front way.

Inspector Murphy stood up as the chief superintendent entered his office and Dekker came straight to the point. "Hanley reckons this is serious. What do you think?"

"I think so too, sir."

"We don't waste time then. What's been done?"

"We've made a search of the school and other possible places, and every house in the road en route to her home has been visited. A record of each visit is there." He lifted a thick wad of papers and let it fall back on to his desk. "Nothing to go on yet. A number of the parents, neighbours and friends have formed a search party. They're out now but I don't think it's particularly well organized."

"How many police officers have we got?"

"Fifty-two, sir, some of them the night shift who have come on early. We've brought all the equipment we could muster at short notice and there are four dog handlers here. A description of the girl has, of course, been circulated."

"Who are the civilians outside, if the other lot are already out?"

"More neighbours and people who have heard about it."

"We can use them. Where's the room you've cleared for it?"

"The parade room. It's not all that big but it's the biggest we've got. There are two internal phones and an outside one there."

"Personal radios?"

16

"There should be enough."

They went into the long narrow parade room with its brown and green paint, noticeboards and plain wooden chairs and tables. Dekker picked up the photograph of the girl and then turned his attention to the three Ordnance Survey maps spread out on the largest table.

"Can I make a suggestion, sir?" said Murphy. "I've had time to think about it."

"Go ahead."

"There are six sergeants here. Divide the map into six parts of fairly equal density and form six squads with a sergeant in charge of each. We can cut the maps up, and each sergeant can then be responsible for his own area."

"Good idea! What about mobiles?"

"Two for each squad and the rest on stand-by. Dog handlers, after the usual procedure, can join in as and when necessary. We'll need the vehicles for flood lighting later and the emergency van can go to any particularly difficult part."

"Let's get started. Get the sergeants in here and I'll brief them. You organize the six groups outside while I'm doing it. What about your other inspector here, were you able to contact him?"

"No. I believe he's gone out for the day."

"Pity. When all this is arranged, you'd better go with the dog section to the parents' home. They'll want something for scent, I believe. Anyway, see the dog people and do what you can for the parents. I suppose their house has been searched?"

"Thoroughly."

Dekker was marking out the map as the sergeants came in and, when he'd finished and had divided it roughly into six sections and lettered each one, he turned to them.

"You all know what this is about. Each one of you will be in charge of a search party and will take a section of the map. It will be your responsibility to make sure that the area entrusted to you is searched thoroughly and you will be held responsible if the child is afterwards found in a place you should have covered. Fortunately a search on this scale is not

17

the sort of thing we've got much practice in, so much will be left to your own common sense and training. Any questions?"

"Private premises and houses, sir?"

"No. Only if you have good reason. If there are any lock-up places you feel ought to be searched, radio in and we'll get the keyholder. We can only go so far tonight. If nothing comes of it by the morning the whole thing will have to be reorganized on a larger scale. You should all have a description of the girl by now. Someone get a pair of scissors, cut up the maps and get started."

Beech Avenue was a quiet, residential area and the detached houses and bungalows were set well back from the road. To Inspector Murphy, who arrived with the police dog handler, it seemed even more quiet than usual, menacingly so.

He went up the path to the Murrays' home, noting the care which had been lavished on the garden, the immaculate paintwork of the double-fronted house, the gleaming windows and quality curtains. A maroon Humber Sceptre stood on the driveway to an opened garage.

He rang the bell and when the door opened he didn't have to be told that the tall man with an athletic build who faced him was the father of the missing girl. There was shock, worry, fear and a suggestion of hopeless inadequacy all rolled into one. The voice matched the expression. "Come in, Inspector. You just caught me. I was about to have another search round."

They followed him into what seemed to be a small occasional lounge and Murray said: "You haven't found her, have you?"

"Not yet but we've organized a full-scale search. I suppose you know that your neighbours have been out for some time?"

"Yes, I saw them go but I couldn't leave my wife. We've already been out. I don't think you'll find her round here."

"Why do you say that?"

"I know my daughter. Somehow someone's driven off with her. It's like those other cases, isn't it?"

With startling suddenness, he sank on to his knees and,

18

hiding his face in his hands, grunted and sobbed pathetically. The inspector and the constable glanced at each other and then, just as suddenly, Murray stood up, wiping his eyes and shaking his head. "Sorry. I've held up until now. My wife mustn't see me do that."

"I do understand, sir, believe me," said the inspector. "But you mustn't give up hope so soon. Where is your wife?"

"She's in the next room with a neighbour. It's no good trying to see her; she can't say anything at all. When she *was* able to, she told everything to your sergeant. We've sent for the doctor."

The inspector turned towards the constable. "Can you let this officer have a few articles of her clothing which have been worn recently?"

"I think so."

Murray left the room and when he returned he was holding a pair of white socks, some pants and a vest. "Will these do?" he said. "They haven't been washed yet. She probably wore—" he choked on the words—"them yesterday."

The sun had almost set when Inspector Murphy got back and a few lights were showing from the police station windows.

Dekker had reorganized things. At a table in one corner, a constable was manning a wireless transmitter which had been brought in, and another constable was sitting by a telephone with the receiver to his ear, taking notes. A large map had appeared on one of the noticeboards and parts of it had been shaded over with a heavy black pencil.

"How did you get on?" asked Dekker.

Murphy grimaced and shook his head. "I've carried a few agony messages in my time but I don't want any more jobs like that. I thought I was hard, but there's something about a strong man breaking down as he did which gets you. Anyway, we've got some scent articles but so far they haven't done any good. The dogs sniffed around her desk at school and showed interest but it would have been a miracle if they had kept it with all the other kids who had been there. Now they've joined the other search parties."

Dekker pointed to the map. "We're getting messages now and again letting us know the ground they've covered—the shaded parts. We've called out three keyholders so far. By the way, I've looked through those reports from your house-to-house check and I see nine of them weren't in."

"That's right. Someone will have to call back."

The loudspeaker burst into life. "Hallo Z from Z4."

"Go ahead Z4," said the constable at the microphone.

"We're in Ferry Lane and we've found a child's black shoe. One of the dogs is more than interested and has led us to the first gate of a bungalow but no further. There's no one at home there. Shall we break in?"

Dekker strode over and, after signalling to the constable, spoke into the microphone. "Chief Superintendent. Yes, break in and make any necessary enquiries in the area. Mark the spot where the shoe was found and leave a constable with it. Have you got that?"

"Roger, sir. Will do."

Dekker and Murphy stared at each other and both went to the map.

"You know the area," said Dekker. "Point it out."

The inspector ran his finger across the map and stopped at Ferry Lane. "It's a quiet road. At one time it ran down to the ferry which crossed the river at Hockstead and it now also leads to the main road. Are you thinking of closing it?"

"I think we'd better. I'll get the traffic van to meet you there with some signs and floodlights. Try and keep the others away from the spot where the shoe was found. Bloody hell! I don't like it! I'm getting on to the CID after I've contacted the ACC and the Chief."

Another inspector came in with something of a flurry and saluted. "I've only just heard, sir. A few more have arrived outside."

"We can use 'em. Tell them to stand by and I'll fill you

20

in," said Dekker and he went to the telephone and rang the Assistant Chief Constable.

Murphy was back again in half an hour, holding a small black shoe, scored along one side and with traces of mud on the heel. "There's no one at home at the bungalow and by the number of letters on the mat it looks as if they've been away for some time. There's no sign of her there."

"Have you sealed off the road?"

"Yes, with diversion signs and lamps and I've had the spot floodlit and roped off."

Dekker nodded and then gave him a sympathetic glance. "Now you've got another rotten job!"

"I know, sir. I'll get it over with," said Murphy and went out to his car again.

Joe Murray was at his front gate, staring fixedly up the road. He stood with his wide, thick shoulders hunched and his hands thrust inside his trouser pockets and, as the car drew up, he moved his head slightly.

When Murphy produced the shoe he took it, turning it over slowly, his face twitching suddenly in his effort to keep control. Pointing to the score mark, he nodded and with difficulty got out the words, "Yes . . . It's hers."

At first glance there was nothing particularly outstanding about Detective-Superintendent Matt Anders. He was a tall, strongly-built man but there are many such in the police service. His hair was grey and receding, his features regular and well balanced: a pleasant face yet one which could easily be lost in a crowd. But few people were in his company for long without realizing that he was far from ordinary.

Unlike a number of his contemporaries, he had achieved promotion in the face of political opposition. His career had been marked by a series of stops and starts, influenced by repeated clashes of personality and his refusal to accept that with some people it was far better to be wrong than right.

Time and again promotion boards passed him over, for

when his name came up there had always been at least one senior officer with a rankling memory. "Good thief-catcher, yes. Good sergeant but more than that—risky! A bit unorthodox at times. Not flexible enough. Liable to offend the wrong people," and so on.

Then Charles Metcalfe had come, a straight-thinking Chief Constable who made a point of finding things out for himself. There was a considerable shake-up and within a short time Anders found himself striding up the ladder until he was now the head of the force CID.

He was told about the disappearance of Angela Murray at five past ten. As he put the phone down, Italy, Lake Como, Bellagio, all seemed a long way away. He and his wife, Elizabeth, had planned the holiday so carefully months ago: just the two of them at an unpretentious lakeside hotel away from the bustle and the crowds. Tomorrow they were due to leave from Heathrow.

There was still a chance, of course, but an instinctive foreboding told him that it was a remote one. It was the finding of the girl's shoe which was particularly ominous. That and the ghastly affair at Coolidge which had kept a Yard squad and fifty other officers fully occupied for the past six months. He was too far away to be in the centre of things but near enough to help with local enquiries. He knew the details well enough.

Four girls between the ages of six and nine had disappeared. Three of them had been found, two in a ditch and one in dense bracken. They had all been sexually assaulted—one atrociously—and suffocated. He had seen the photographs and the relative files and, hardened as he had necessarily become, it had preyed on his mind. He had said little about it to Elizabeth.

Now he and his officers could find themselves in the centre of things. They wouldn't be able to tell for certain until they had found her, and find her they must as soon as possible.

He rang Detective Chief Inspector Carver and Sergeant

Hudson and explained briefly, giving them instructions to meet him within fifteen minutes in his office.

Elizabeth reacted immediately he went into the sitting-room. After twenty-eight years, she could read every changing flicker on his face. The telephone call hadn't been a social one: something serious had happened.

"It's a nine-year-old girl missing from Forebridge. Sorry, dear, but I've got to go down there."

"Oh no!" she said and he knew she wasn't thinking only of their holiday.

He went into the hall and collected his briefcase. Then he kissed her on the cheek. "I'll let you know as soon as I can," he said and hurried out to his car.

Carver and Hudson were waiting for him.

Carver had the build of an agile, heavyweight wrestler, his muscles bulging under his immaculate brown suit. He had a long, thick neck, a slightly misshapen nose and intelligent eyes which were very blue and deceptively mild. Deep creases in his forehead gave him an air of perpetual surprise when in fact he was rarely surprised at anything.

By contrast, Hudson just about made the height minimum for the force and he was inclined to be sloppily dressed. He was patient, perceptive and quiet-mannered but very occasionally—and for no apparent reason at all—he could be as obstinate as a mule.

Carver said: "I've been on to Forebridge since you rang, sir. It doesn't look good."

"No," said Anders. "It doesn't. Unless we've got an imitator, it seems that chummy has decided to move farther afield. But . . . she may turn up."

"D'you really think so? Now we've found the shoe?"

Anders sat at his desk. "Not alive, Fred. I don't think they'll find her alive." He slid a sheet of foolscap paper to Carver. "Make a note of the things I want you to do. Sergeant Hudson can come with me."

Carver produced his pen and waited.

23

"Contact the scene-of-crime crew on call and tell them to report with their equipment to Forebridge as soon as they can. Get someone from Traffic to go to Coolidge and bring back specimen questionnaires they've been using. Ring Chief Superintendent Jordan there and put him in the picture. Draft an order cancelling all leave for CID and contact as many as you can and tell them to go to Forebridge. Arrange for as many aides as you can from uniform branch and warn the Traffic and Dog Section that we shall probably need all the frogmen and dogs they've got. Cancel anything else which can be cancelled and ring the chief. Tell him what we're doing and give him my compliments. Tell him if this girl doesn't turn up safe and sound by the morning, I want his permission to treat this as a murder enquiry and to liaise with the officers at Coolidge."

Carver, who had been furiously writing his own type of shorthand, went on scribbling and then looked up. "What about the Press?"

"It may be premature but lay on a conference for ten o'clock tomorrow morning at Forebridge."

Anders stood up and glanced at his watch. "Ten forty-five. We won't be there before eleven-thirty. We'd better get going." He paused at the door. "There's one other thing. If this develops as I think it may do, I shall want you down there with me. We'll get a DCI and a DI from a Division to take over here."

Hudson drove the CID Hillman Hunter, and Anders sat thinking and listening to the messages which crackled to and fro on the car radio.

It was unwise, he knew, to get personally involved in anything like this but, with the prospect of finding a small, pathetic body and of knowing the agony of the parents, it was difficult not to.

A plaintive voice from the mobile canteen stated that they were having difficulty in reaching one of the search parties and after a brief delay a different route was suggested to them.

Anders glanced at Hudson who, sensing that his chief could be in one of his thoughtful, unconversational moods, had maintained a tactful silence.

"Weren't you at Forebridge for a time?" asked Anders.

"For a couple of years, sir, bar a few weeks. That was over fifteen years ago, before I joined the CID."

"I don't know it as well as most other parts of the county. What sort of place is it?"

"When I was there it was a semi-rural town. Used to have a cattle market but they packed that up years ago. And it's grown too—sort of spread. They've filled up a lot of the vacant spaces, mostly with pricy residential property. There's also a fairly large council estate. It's still not as big as Coolidge though."

"Have they left the old town alone?"

"More or less, but they've developed behind it—a parallel road with modern shops, including a supermarket. I liked it better as it was. A nice bit of river runs round the south side."

"What do the people do for a living?"

"Commute mostly. All that's left of the old brickfields are a couple of disused quarries."

Anders glanced at the speedometer. "Is this as fast as you can go?" he asked and Hudson, who had allowed the car to slow a little while they were talking, put his foot down again and concentrated on his driving.

Soon they turned off the main road and the headlights swept across the battered rough stone wall surrounding a once-stately residence which marked the road to Forebridge.

When they drew into the police station yard, lights were streaming from most of the windows of the old red-brick building and there was an air of tension about the whole place. A typewriter was clattering as they entered. The officer at the desk paused and looked up. "In the parade room, sir."

Anders nodded and they passed through. Wireless conversation greeted them from the open door and when they went in Dekker, with his jacket off and collar undone, turned from the map he had been studying. Murphy was drinking coffee and a constable was making up some sort of a log by a tele-phone.

"Am I glad to see you, Matt!" said Dekker. "We've been doing all we can but I'm sorry to say that it's now a job for the CID. Inspector Murphy had better explain."

Murphy stood up. "Like some coffee while you're listening, sir?"

"No, thanks all the same. Give it to us in detail."

Murphy gave it to him—very cogently Anders thought—and, when they came to the finding of the shoe, he looked at it and frowned. "It's a positive identification?"

"Practically. Mr. Murray recognized the scratch mark down the side and it's her size and similar to those she was wearing."

"Has the area been cordoned off?"

"We've done that and it's been floodlit."

"I'd beter get down there then. When scene-of-crime arrive, send them along, will you?"

Anders let his eyes wander over Dekker's clothes. "What? Did they drag you from a party, Bill?"

"Not quite, but I was on my way to one. Weren't you going on holiday tomorrow?"

"I was. But I've a feeling we can forget about parties and holidays for a bit. See you later."

They reached Ferry Lane and had to stop to remove some of the hurricane lamps stretched across the road on each side of the police "No entry" sign. Then they drove on and, round-ing a bend, saw the distant blaze of light.

Hudson stopped well short of the area and they went on foot. Two ghostly, helmeted figures emerged from the shadows and a sergeant materialized and saluted. "I heard you were on the way, sir, so I came back to explain." Anders observed the tripod-held flood lamps with their pipes trailing to the butane gas cylinders. "Thank you, Sergeant. How far does this go?"

"A hundred feet either side of where the shoe was found. We've marked the spot with a cone. The centre lamp is portable so you can move it around as you want."

"Is that the place where nobody's at home?" said Anders,

pointing towards the dark outline of a bungalow showing over a hedge.

"We couldn't find anything there, sir, but in the last ten minutes we've discovered that it belongs to a Mr. and Mrs. Wemsley who went on holiday last week and won't be coming back until next week. A Mr. Short who lives about half a mile up the road told us. He's keeping an eye on the place for them."

"Has he got the address where they're staying?"

"Yes, sir. I've made a note of it."

"In the morning get the police of wherever it is to call on them and take them to their station, so that they can phone here and we'll explain. We can secure the place so there's no need to spoil their holiday."

"Do you want us to secure it?"

"Not until we've had another look round."

"Right, sir. If there's nothing else, I'll get back to my search party."

"How far have you covered?"

"About a square half-mile, sir."

"Thank you, Sergeant."

The sergeant saluted and disappeared into the blackness behind the lights. Then they heard his car turning in the road.

They were carefully examining the ground near the amber cone when an approaching car heralded the arrival of the scene-of-crime officers.

"We're lucky, sir," said one of them cheerfully, glancing up at the night sky. "Need good weather for anything like this," and Anders checked an impulse to ask him if he enjoyed searching for murdered children. "Let's see," he said, "if that last course you went on will produce some results. I don't want anything missed. Shots and casts identified with exact locations. Draw a plan and section it off. Soil samples from all round, identified on the plan." He pointed to the bungalow. "Go through it and all round it, and when you've finished clear the road and arrange to have the place properly secured."

* * *

Dawn came and the searchers, reduced to less than half the original number, wearily ploughed on. By six o'clock Anders and Dekker were conferring back at the station and it was decided to call them in and begin again.

"I've about had it," said Dekker, "and I've got to get back. What about you?"

"I'll get things organized here to make a fresh start. It'll be a tidy old job."

"You'll have the early shift now and I'll tell the others to get back as soon as possible," said Dekker. "They're all yours. I don't think I can do any more for you." Then he rubbed his eyes and yawned, and with a wave of his hand he went out.

Anders stared at the map with its futile shaded areas and thought briefly of Lake Como. Then, with a resigned shrug, he reached for the telephone.

Carver's voice sounded several tones deeper. "I've told the Chief and he's leaving it to you. Whatever you want, he'll back you. Says he'll be down during the morning. It's bad, is it?"

"Looks that way. Here's another list for you. Marker tapes— get plenty. Get on to the OC of the REME at Rittle and explain the position. Tell him I'd like as many men as he can spare, to get here by eleven. We may need them all day. Beds and bedding for you, me and one other at least. You've fixed everything else?"

"All done. You'll have it all by nine, I should say, or most of it."

"Good. After the Press have had the photograph of the girl, I want you to arrange for it to be blown up to crown size and have say two hundred posters printed. Did you get the questionnaire?"

"Yes, and I've adapted it. Is that the lot?"

"I wish I could think it was. Hand over all you can and get along here."

CHAPTER 3

His name was Peter Mellish. He was thirty-six years old, just on six feet tall and strongly built. His dark shiny hair was short by prevailing standards but still long enough and thick enough to spread in springy waves from a well-shaped forehead. His features were firm and regular and his dark eyes, under prominent straight brows, steady and rarely blinking.

There was a hint of recklessness about him which most women found attractive. Dogs didn't take to him.

He was also a drifter. Not the vagrant type but a drifter all the same, rarely stopping in one place or in one job for more than a few months at a time. But he was remarkably skilled with his hands, turning with equal success to anything from plumbing to tiling, roofing or carpentry—or even to playing the piano which he did by ear in a quite professional and individualistic style. He was also clever with a camera and in the processing of film. He was therefore soon in demand wherever he went and certainly as much as he wanted to be.

His longest spell in one job had been in the Merchant Navy over ten years previously. Marriage had never entered into his plans, although only luck and the availability of contraceptives had prevented his making a considerable contribution to the population in various scattered parts of the world. Conversely, and in his own way, he had helped to reduce it.

Now he was home again with his mother, an ageing but sturdy woman who referred to him as "my Pete" and, in return for the generous allowance which gave her unlimited opportunities for bingo and beer, she fawned and fussed over him, not noticing when she did so the sardonic amusement which sometimes appeared in his eyes.

They lived in a council house on the fringe of the new town and this had been the second longest stay Mellish had had in one place since his schooldays. Nine months he had been there, and he would have left before this if it hadn't been for Mavis Stringer. He had met her when he had been engaged by a local builder to tile her bathroom over six months previously, and when he had first seen her, he had thought—not bad, not bad at all, but probably a bit snooty. In a rather exaggerated county voice she had explained what she wanted and had then left him to it.

Later she had brought him some coffee and cakes on a tray and had asked him one or two questions about himself. Cautiously he had felt his way but before she left he had, by subtle inference and an occasional cheeky smile, let it be known that he was willing if she was.

He hadn't pushed it though. On the following day he had been quick to note the change of dress style and the added care she had taken with her make-up. Her blouse allowed for a distinct cleavage and her skirt left a provocative view of well-shaped knees when she sat down. He had wondered what her husband was like—she had mentioned him only once—but it didn't take him long to guess that she was hungry for something different.

Over the next break for coffee their conversation had become more intimate and his graphic accounts of places he had visited abroad seemed to intrigue her. Suddenly she had said: "And you've never wanted to marry or settle down?"

The quick smile had evaporated and he had looked at her

seriously. "I don't know about that. Maybe I haven't yet met anyone who was interested and who could satisfy me. If either party can't get it right, they'll go on looking somewhere else, so what would have been the point?"

She had stared back at him and her lips had parted slightly as he had leaned closer to her. Still she had stared at him until his mouth was inches from hers and then she had closed her eyes.

After that it had been easy, and what he had said without sincerity as a tempting bait, he found to be true. She *had* satisfied him. Christ, had she? You could never tell with a woman until you had her undressed. She was fantastic, bloody fantastic. Firm breasts with hard nipples—you couldn't tell that beforehand, and shape—the right shape all over. Even then you could never tell until they switched on their machinery. She did that all right, and with a difference which made all the difference as far as he was concerned. She enjoyed the sadistic touches. She wanted to be hurt. She had writhed and gasped and almost screamed.

Before the tiling job was finished she was clay in his hands, and because she almost satisfied his perverted instincts, he arranged to meet her again, and again, but always on his terms. They were to take her car. She was to pick him up while out visiting or shopping, and afterwards they were to go where he wanted. In a way it was even better in the car; the bedroom was almost too easy.

He first suggested driving the car around himself when she went to the hairdresser near Coolidge. "You'll be about an hour," he'd said, "and I'll be waiting for you when you come out." She had hesitated fractionally and then agreed.

Lately they had been able to manage an evening now and again as well, and the screened patch behind the bushes in the old quarry had been the most suitable spot so far.

As he brushed his hair in front of his bedroom mirror, he wondered what had happened, what her husband had said and what he had done. He hadn't seen him, but she had and had suddenly gone limp just as she was getting herself really wound

31

up. Perhaps it would end now! He didn't like that idea at all. It was for him to decide when and where they should finish with each other.

It was nearly nine when he went down. A smell and sizzling of frying bacon came from the kitchen. His mother heard him and put her head round the door. "Two eggs as usual, Pete?"

"Yes, Ma, two eggs as usual." He was glancing through the morning papers when she brought in his breakfast. "Police were about all last night," she said. "Some girl missing."

"Oh, that's what it was."

"What you doing today?"

"One or two things, nothing much."

"They were wondering down at the Bull if you might come and give us a tune. They do like the way you play that Lara tune thing."

He finished swallowing a mouthful of egg and bacon and nodded slowly. "I might do that."

"Do try, Pete," said his mother and then she hesitated in the doorway and glanced at him furtively. "Of course we'll understand if you can't. You don't happen to have a coupla quid to spare, I suppose?"

His mouth turned down at the ends. "What happened to the extra fiver I gave you the day before yesterday?"

"Well, you know..."

"I know. You had a bad session at the hall. Don't you ever get tired of that?"

"I win sometimes, Pete, and it's exciting."

He felt in his back pocket, pulled out a thick roll of notes and, extracting two, looked at them thoughtfully. Then he flicked them across the table so that one fell on to the floor. She picked it up and the one on the table. "Thank you, Pete. You're a good boy."

Half an hour later he rang Mavis Stringer from a call box. "You on your own?"

Her voice sounded different, insecure. "Yes. He's gone to the office."

"What did he say?"

"Nothing. I wish he had."

"He must have said *something?*"

"Not until I did. I asked him what he was going to do and he said he didn't know. That's all. I didn't see him go this morning. Peter! Can't we go away somewhere. I've got about five hundred in the bank and money in a building society. Can't we?"

He frowned at his reflection in the phone booth mirror. "Let's talk about it. When can I see you?"

"This afternoon? I've got a fitting with my dressmaker and I can pick you up at three."

"All right. Usual place then."

"Peter! Are you sure you love me?"

"Of course I do, only I prefer actions to words."

"I'll see you at three."

They both waited for the other to put the phone down and in the end he decided for them.

He went back to his red Mini and sat thinking for some time before he drove off. The idea of going away with her was ludicrous but he hadn't yet had his fill. He would have to stall her.

In the afternoon he made sure he was on time but she was there ahead of him. She gave him a tentative smile as he got in, and when she drove off he put his hand on her knee. "Feeling better?" he said.

She glanced sideways at him, her face serious and slightly drawn. "I do, I suppose, now you're here."

"You only suppose?"

"It was a shock—and if only he'd gone off the deep end about it and we'd had a scene! But I don't know what he thinks or what he intends to do."

He decided to play an ace. "It's not easy to say this, but I want to know what's best for *you*. If you'd be happier in the long run, I'll fade out of the picture."

33

His hand moved up her thigh as he said it and for a few moments she remained silent, swallowing and blinking to keep back the tears. Then she said: "God, Peter, don't say that! I couldn't bear not to be with you again."

"I was dreading you might have had second thoughts."

She felt for his hand and squeezed it and for half a mile neither of them spoke. Then he said: "What you said about us going away together—it sounds fine except for one thing. I've got to be able to give you more than I could now."

"It wouldn't matter. You'd get something."

"Something isn't good enough. But there might be a chance for me, I think, in Newcastle. I could have had it before if I'd promised to settle. Probably a partnership in it—with a friend of mine."

"A partnership? Oh, Peter, what would you be doing?"

"It's a building firm started up a few years ago and business came in faster than they expected. I wouldn't be surprised if the offer is still open. I'll write today. No, I'll phone."

"I've never been to Newcastle. What's it like there?"

"It suited me all right. It's got some posh residential areas and there's some good country round it."

"It all sounds too good to be true..." Her voice trailed off. "If only it weren't for George!"

"I know how you feel but in the long run you'll be doing him a good turn. After all, you can't be suited to each other and it'll give him a chance as well."

"I suppose so."

"But on no account say anything until we're ready. It could ruin everything."

They were slowing down.

"Where are you going?" he asked.

"The next turning. My dressmaker lives down there."

"Hold it! Can you stop a minute?"

She pulled in.

"How long will you be?" he asked.

"About half an hour. I wasn't going to stop outside her house."

"Make it an hour and I'll try and get through to Newcastle now. It might take a bit of time. I can pick you up here, or nearer if you like."

"Could you? D'you know where there's a phone?"

"I'll find one. What do you think? I'll wait here for you if you like, but it would be nice to know."

"No, Peter, please! *Do* try and find out now if you can. I'll walk from here."

When she got out he slid across to the driving seat and glanced at his watch. "I'll be back here not later than half past four."

He watched her go and waved, and as she looked back she held up a hand with two fingers crossed.

Then he pulled slowly away, trying to think where might be the best hunting ground at this time of day, and feeling the controlled excitement growing inside him again.

They would be coming out of school about now, but that wouldn't be any good—too many of them together. Maybe the Collis Road area, a lot of kids round there played hookey!

He stopped at a major road and two police cars went by, one behind the other, and as he crossed over he saw a large police van approaching from the right.

He drove on with more purpose, threading his way through the streets until he came to a poorer part of the town.

Here were rows of terraced houses with front doors which opened straight on to the pavement.

He passed a brick wall with a worn and undecipherable slogan painted on it in crude red letters. Then, round the corner by another wall and hidden from windows, were three children, two girls of about seven and a coloured boy with dark, frizzy hair who couldn't be much older.

One of the girls, in a light blue dress with a blue bow on her hair, was walking near the kerb.

He drew up alongside and he smiled. "Can you tell me the way to Sethley Park?"

They all turned and pointed, and the girl with the bow said: "Over there."

"Is it far?"

"No, not far."

He opened the front passenger door. "Look, d'you think you could get in and show me? I'm in a hurry."

The girl with the bow clambered in and he pulled the door shut. She smiled at her friends as he drove off and he thought: It's worked again! Ask them to do something, tell them you're in a hurry and they forget. But the other times they'd been on their own. Her friends? Hardly any chance they'd take his number. They didn't suspect anything so why should they?

He drove faster now and the girl said: "You've gone past it," as if she were scolding him. Glancing down at her he gave her another smile. "It's all right, dear. I'm going to make a call first now I know where it is. I'll take you back. You don't mind going for a short ride, do you?"

"I don't know," she said uncertainly.

In five minutes they had reached the common and he turned on to a wide track. He turned again to a narrow track, almost hidden by an abundance of straggling ferns, and stopped in a small clearing. The girl was staring round her and he got out quickly and opened her door. "Come on, dear. I want to show you something."

Her eyes were fixed on him and she seemed frozen with fear. "Come on," he said and pulled her out of her seat.

A few yards from the car, he was dragging her along with one hand clamped over her mouth when a rather strident female voice said: "What are you doing with that child?"

Within seconds he calculated and decided. He could deal with the woman but there might be someone with her or nearby. Without turning round, he swung the girl so that he was between her and the woman behind him, and then he let her go. Pointing along the narrowing path ahead, he said: "Go on! Get back to your mother and don't run away again!"

The child stood there for a moment, urine running down her leg where she had wetted herself and then, released from her paralysing fear, she ran away.

Casually but with a look of feigned annoyance on his face, he turned and nodded at the woman, who stood with her feet apart, eyeing him suspiciously. He put her in the "huntin', shootin'" class: middle-aged with a severe hair style and dressed in brown tweeds. She had wide hips and thick legs and her heavy shoes were meant for walking. A fawn labrador was at the end of the lead she held and it too regarded him with obvious dislike.

He sauntered to the car and, standing in front of the number plate, leaned on the bonnet and blew through his mouth. "What a game I've had finding her. Little devil, she's always doing that, running off. Her mother's worried sick."

The woman didn't move her head but her eyes darted from him to the distant path. He was just thinking up a reason why, if he'd been so worried, he had let the girl go again when she said "Oh!" and hurried away in the direction taken by the child.

For a few moments he looked round and listened in case anybody else was about, and then he got into the car again and, starting the engine, ploughed back along the path to the wider stretch.

It had been a close shave! He congratulated himself on the way he had dealt with the situation. He would be all right for a time but if the woman or the child's mother went to the police they might get a description of the car. After this, he couldn't use it or go in it.

He checked his watch and saw that he had been just over half an hour. Would it be best to leave the car where he had said he would wait for her? He could put a note to her on the steering-wheel. But no! If by chance the police did get his number quickly, they might spot the car before she got back and they would see the note. Better idea would be to wait across the road from it and join her when she returned.

This is what he did and while he strolled along the road, keeping the car in view, he entertained the idea of moving on again, going to a new locality, perhaps another ship. Then he saw the danger in that. If he left the district suddenly, he could immediately come under suspicion. As long as they couldn't link him with the car, he felt confident that he could brazen it out. He would have to keep Mavis happy until things had quietened down. Of course the woman or the kid mightn't say anything, but it was as well to be prepared.

She appeared suddenly and, seeing the empty car, looked around in a confused fashion until she saw him. He opened the driver's door for her and gave her a squeeze as she got in.

"I was only about fifteen minutes after all," he said, "so I came back and left the car here and went for a walk."

"Did you get through?"

He went round to the passenger seat. "Yes. Frank's on holiday but I spoke to his partner and it sounds hopeful."

"What did he say?"

"Funny really, he said they were only talking about me last week and he reckons Frank will be dead keen. They've got more than they can manage."

"That's marvellous," she said, and then her face seemed to cloud over. "Are you really sure, Peter? You know I'm older than you?"

"You don't look it," he lied. "Here, you do mean it, don't you? You're not going to let me down?"

"Of course not. But George has never really done me any harm."

"I was thinking about him." He forced a worried frown of concern. "This car, I don't like to go in it now. It is his, isn't it?"

"Yes, although I use it most."

"It didn't seem to matter when he didn't know, but now, I feel..."

"I think that's rather nice of you, Peter."

"I must be getting soft. Anyway, in future I'll meet you and pick you up in my car. Only we'll have to find somewhere and get out. It isn't big enough. Now, in view of what's happened, I'm going to leave you."

"But I thought..."

He looked quickly through the back window and then fondled her breasts as he kissed her. "Tomorrow, I'll give you a ring in the morning. Now this has come up, I'm going to make a couple of calls to collect some money owing to me, and I did promise to write today confirming my suggestion."

CHAPTER 4

After Dekker had left, Anders freshened himself with a wash-down in cold water and made a mental note to send for several changes of clothing. Then, with Sergeant Hudson, he occupied the following hour going over events from the beginning.

A list of the Murrays' relatives and close friends had been obtained and these had already been checked in case for some reason the child had gone there. Inspector Murphy and Sergeant Gisling had been in no doubt at all that neither of the parents was in any way concerned, but Anders had to see for himself and personally eliminate as far as he could even the remotest of possibilities. Interviewing parents in such cases was always a harrowing task. You had to compromise between discouraging false hope and avoiding black despair.

Ten minutes with Joe Murray convinced him that Murphy and Gisling had not been deceived. Murray was still in the clothes he had come home in. His face was haggard; his tie was hanging loose and his open shirt collar showed sweat and dirt. The rest of his clothing was fouled with recently-acquired dirt and dust.

A policewoman was with Mrs. Murray and, after a brief consultation with her, Anders decided it was pointless to try to interview the still-sedated woman.

As he left he tried to place Murray; the face, the build and the name rang a bell. Then it came to him. About ten years ago he had been a first class rugby player, due for international honours until he had broken a leg.

He returned to the station, snatched a quick breakfast and prepared for the press conference.

It might have been a gathering for a funeral. Hardened pressmen who had seen it all before at Coolidge had seen it too often. They were sickened by it and the grim prospect of more to come. The proceedings were subdued and there were none of the usual tricky questions designed to extract sensational copy. Nobody wanted this sort of sensation. Consequently it didn't take long and, with copies of the girl's photograph, they left, some of them with thoughts of their own children returning from school or waiting for them at home.

So that normal activities could continue undisturbed at Forebridge police station, they took over the Forebridge Labour Hall for use as a Murder Headquarters. Extra land lines were installed—the Post Office expediting matters with commendable efficiency—and all the necessary equipment was collected for what was obviously going to be a prolonged investigation.

A small side room was cleared and beds installed for those officers who, for an indefinite period, would be on continuous duty.

Five hundred troops arrived, earlier than expected, and were divided into five parties to link with the police and several hundred volunteers. Each party was under the leadership of a police inspector and they departed with all necessary tools, maps, personal radios and hundreds of yards of white tape to mark the ground they would cover.

Most of the town had already been searched, and it was

decided to concentrate on the surrounding countryside, particularly the common and the wooded area to the north of it. Each party had a number of dogs and utility vehicles for carrying equipment and food. There were at least a hundred square miles to cover and not a ditch or crevice to go unchecked. It could take a long time.

A special team of frogmen was despatched to the river and a crew of a newly-acquired, cumbersome-looking vehicle, which had huge tires designed for boggy ground, made for the marshy area on the low-lying side of Forebridge. A helicopter provided by the RAF circled overhead, ready to provide an aerial link with the searchers on the ground.

At two o'clock Chief Inspector Carver arrived and Anders decided to allow himself the luxury of a few hours' sleep.

It was five minutes past four when he awoke and, as the cobwebs cleared, he was conscious of Carver speaking from the next room, on the telephone it seemed. There was some urgency in his voice. "Yes. I've got it. A telephone box at the junction of Common Road and Red Lane. Stay there, Mrs. Conway, and a car will be along in a few minutes."

Anders went to the doorway as Carver said to the wireless operator: "You got that location and name?"

"Yes, sir."

"Get a car there urgently to bring them back here." Carver picked up the telephone and dialled. "Information Room." He waited, tapping his fingers impatiently on the table. "Information Room? Chief Inspector Carver at Forebridge. Urgent message for immediate circulation. Description of man and car, attempted abduction of child on common, north of Forebridge, within last half-hour. Five feet ten, well-built, in pale blue shirt with open-neck collar, pale blue slacks, tight-fitting, dark hair, thick and brushed back, about thirty to thirty-five, good-looking. Car: saloon, green, new-looking, number believed to contain an 'H' and a three."

He listened while they repeated it and then said: "Right. We'll get someone from here as well." He was striding to the map when he realized that Anders had appeared. "I was just going to wake you, sir. Did you hear that?"

"Yes. Any chance of it being the Murray child?"

"No. The name's Peggy Finney and she lives in East Street."

"What more is there?"

"This Mrs. Conway was walking across the common when she saw a man dragging a child along and his car standing by. When she challenged him, he let the girl go and made out it was his daughter. Something about him scared her and she went after the child who was in a bit of a state, and it appears that the man was no more the kid's father than I am. I left it there to save wasting more time."

Anders shook his head sadly. "Murray, poor bugger! I was still hoping. How did you come to get the call through here?"

"For some reason she rang the station and as soon as they realized what it was about they had the sense to transfer it."

They went to the map and Carver ran his finger over it. "That's where she called from so she must have seen him somewhere in the part of the common they went through this morning."

"I'm going to have a quick wash," said Anders. "Find Policewoman Reeves and when the woman and child get here, she can soften the child up a bit before we see her."

The phone rang again and the constable who answered it turned his head towards them. "Message from Headquarters, sir. A woman has just rung on '999' to say she's heard that her daughter has been picked up by a man in a car."

"What's her address?" asked Anders and Carver in unison.

"Twenty-five East Street, a Mrs. Finney. They've sent a car along."

"That's a relief," said Anders; "for one horrible moment I thought it might be another one! Contact Sergeant Hudson and tell him to get his skates on with his photokit outfit."

"He's on the air," said the officer at the radio, and pushed forward the transmitter switch. "From MHQ. Urgent message for Sergeant Hudson..."

* * *

43

Mrs. Conway arrived with Peggy Finney, who clung to her and stared at them with wide, suspicious eyes, her face streaked with tear stains and her clothing dishevelled and grubby.

With a little coaxing, she took the policewoman's hand and looked back over her shoulder as she was led away to an adjoining room. Mrs. Conway, with her labrador on a lead, strode majestically to the seat Carver had pulled back for her, and opened the proceedings. "Is it this man, the one at Coolidge?" she said.

Anders glanced at the policewoman stenographer who sat at the next table and she switched on the tape recorder.

"It is possible," he said. "If so, we're all very grateful to you. I'm Detective-Superintendent Anders and this is Detective Chief Inspector Carver. To save valuable time, will you tell us from the beginning what happened? We'll ask questions afterwards."

She gave a businesslike nod and told them.

"You've described this man," said Anders when she had finished. "Can you think of anything else about him? What about his voice?"

"Nothing remarkable about it. Ordinary, but pleasant sounding."

"Any accent?"

"Nothing definite. Local, I should say, but he didn't sound uneducated."

"Any mannerisms? Any way of looking at you or any movement of hands—or something like that?"

She frowned and then shut her eyes. "I wouldn't say he had any mannerisms. But there was a fixed look about his eyes."

"You mean he stared?"

"Not exactly. I don't know how to describe it. His eyes had a fixed look as if they were false ones he could move about when he wanted to."

"If you saw the car again, would you recognize it?"

"I think I should. In fact my brother-in-law has one very similar." She jerked at the lead as the dog started to explore Carver's trousers for interesting smells.

"And you would recognize the man again?"

"Most certainly, even if he disguised himself as an archbishop. I'd know those eyes again."

Anders stood up and beckoned to Sergeant Hudson. "Thank you, Mrs. Conway. What you have told us has been recorded and a statement will be prepared for you to sign. If you will be good enough to go with this officer, he would like you to help him to produce a photo likeness of the man you saw."

When she moved from her chair, her rather overweight dog lumbered to its feet and took a passing sniff at Carver as they followed Hudson from the room.

Mrs. Finney had arrived, a fair woman with a thin neck and too much make-up. With her was a small, coloured boy with frizzy hair and a serious demeanour.

"Where is she?" she said and her mouth set in a thin, straight line.

Anders immediately placed her as anti-police and resentful that her daughter had become involved. "She's with a policewoman at the moment," he said.

"Little bitch! Wait till I get her home!"

"I suppose you do *want* her to go home?"

She stared at him truculently. "Of course I do. What d'you mean?"

"I mean that if you do, you're lucky to be able to. Another few minutes and she would most probably have been dead, after having been savaged like the children at Coolidge. Think of that, Mrs. Finney, and think too of the policemen who are working night and day to prevent it happening again."

Her eyes wavered and then she shrugged her thin shoulders.

Anders turned to the boy and said kindly: "You were with Peggy?"

"Yes, sir."

"Do you think you can help us make up a picture of this man?"

"I might."

"Good. What name shall we call you by?"

"Roddy. Roddy Temple."

45

"That's short for Roderick, isn't it?"

"Yes, sir."

"All right, Roddy. You wait here and the sergeant will see you soon. Perhaps you'd like a cup of tea, Mrs. Finney?"

"Thanks."

"And you, Roddy?"

"Yes, please, sir."

"Sit down then and I'll fix it for you," said Anders and left them, to join the policewoman and the girl.

He smiled at the child and said: "Hallo, Peggy!"

"Hallo!"

The policewoman stood up and handed him a sheet of detailed information. When he'd read it, she said: "You'll notice, sir, that when he asked the way to the park, he used the local pronunciation "Selly" and not the way it's spelt—'Sethley'."

"Full marks for bringing that out! Now, as soon as Sergeant Hudson has finished, help him with the car pictures and see if you can get the make and type identified."

At 7:30 p.m. Anders arrived at the plain, solid-looking building at Coolidge which normally housed the Townswomen's Guild, the Boy Scouts and one or two local clubs, and which was now being used as a Murder Headquarters.

Jordan, a big man with heavy features, grey hair and a gravel voice, was waiting for him. They were well acquainted, having shared a room while at a Wakefield detective course in the early days, as well as having liaised several times since then and, of course, recently.

They went into a small side room away from the paraphernalia of phones, documents and filing systems on which a number of male and female officers were engaged.

"From what you told me on the phone," said Jordan, "this is the first real break we've had."

Anders opened his briefcase and took out the photokit picture. "Mrs. Conway and the two children all helped to compile separate pictures. Then each, on their own, was shown the three pictures and without help from the others they all agreed

46

that this was the best likeness. They were all in fact very similar. I think we've now got a good one."

Jordan studied the picture and, after turning it over and reading the description, he stretched over his desk and produced another photograph. "That's the one we had made up. They're not unlike, are they? And I'll tell you what is significant: one of the girls who helped make this one said the man asked her where Capel Terrace was and suggested that she show him as he was in a hurry."

"Then it must be chummy," said Anders. "Why not let your children see this? Perhaps they'll agree that it's a better likeness."

"That's what I had in mind. What else have you got?"

Anders pulled out some glossy advertising brochures of Austin and Hillman saloons. "Mrs. Conway thinks it's the Austin 1800 and the children think it might be the Hillman. They all agree that it's more or less the colour as shown for the Austin. The children have no idea of the number but Mrs. Conway is sure it has an 'H' and a three in it. He's obviously a local man. I told you about the way he pronounced 'Sethley'?"

Jordan slumped back in his chair and rubbed the heel of his hand over his forehead. "We must catch him this time, Matt. Between you and me, I'm nearly all in. Six months we've been going. Every house within miles has been visited, every occupant questioned. At least sixty thousand car files, including yours, have been checked and umpteen useless and bogus leads followed up. So far it's got us nowhere."

"How much sleep have you had?"

"A few hours each week. But we've got to keep going until we get him. And don't you let on I've spoken like this. It's a relief to be able to just for once, without letting the others know."

"I can guess how you feel and I suppose I've got it to come."

"Half of my men haven't had a break to speak of." Jordan took a deep breath and got up. "Anyway, perhaps you've at last come up with something. Have you got yourself organized?"

"Not yet like you have."

"Anything you want from here?"

"I'll use the same filing and cross-indexing system and I'd like to check on that again. Perhaps you could send someone over?"

"You can have the sergeant who's been running it. He's an expert by now. He'll probably get on your nerves a bit. Once he starts, he keeps fussing over it like an old hen."

"As long as he lays the right eggs, he can fuss as much as he likes. Keep the pictures and I'll let you have some more later. It'll be on television tonight and in the papers tomorrow."

"After that," said Jordan, "watch out for anybody leaving the district. But I don't have to tell you!"

When he got home after leaving Mavis Stringer, Mellish changed into a pair of easy-fitting brown trousers and a fawn shirt. Then he rolled up the light blue slacks and shirt he had been wearing and went downstairs. His mother was still out— no doubt feverishly watching her bingo card, he thought.

The black plastic rubbish bag provided by the Corporation was housed in a dustbin in the back yard. Tomorrow they would bring a new one and they would take this one away and sling it into the back of a dustcart with umpteen others to be pummelled and compressed by the screw thing at the back. The bag was nearly full and he emptied some of the contents on to a newspaper and pushed the slacks and shirt to the bottom before tipping the rubbish back again and pressing it down.

This, as far as he could see, was all he could do for the moment, and he congratulated himself on his foresight. Now there was only the car to connect him, and he doubted if the woman or the kid had seen enough of it to give much of a description, but it would be as well to work on Mavis a bit more.

His mother came back just after six and he could tell by her face that she had done fairly well. He also knew that she wouldn't admit it. "How did it go?" he asked.

48

"About got my money back, but I was unlucky, Pete. Only wanted number forty-five on the last card for the big prize."

"Who got it?"

"Oh!" She was thinking what to say. "Some bitch I've seen there before. Doesn't go very often. You coming to the Bull tonight, Pete?"

He gave it serious thought. "Yes. That's not a bad idea," he said.

He put on a figured tie which matched his shirt and surveyed himself in the mirror, turning once or twice to get a different view. The shirt, with its deep pointed collar, sat well on his wide shoulders, and his trousers fitted smoothly over his firm waist and hips. He went downstairs and called out: "It's gone half past seven, Ma. If you're ready I'll run you down there."

"That's nice, Pete. An extra treat. I shan't be a minute."

He waited patiently while she fussed about and searched for her handbag and then, with a consideration he rarely showed her, he settled her in the front passenger seat.

When they reached the pub, he ushered her in and went straight to the bar, ordering her a large gin and tonic and a mild and bitter for himself. He didn't have to buy any more drinks after that. The younger Mrs. Thomas put her arm half round his neck. "Come on, Pete. What about getting on the piano?"

Apart from a few pauses to drink his beer and for a visit to the lavatory, he played continuously until closing time, giving them a mixture of old and new. When they didn't join in, he excelled himself while they listened appreciatively and when they did he played mechanically, hearing the discordant voices in the background while he thought of other things.

Their hearty rendering of "Waltzing Matilda" took him back to Brisbane and the girl—about fifteen she must have been—he had tracked across waste ground on the edge of the town. Suspecting his intention, she had run in panic and when he had decided to move in he found her scratched and bleeding from the brambles and coarse brush. He had left her, knowing that he would be miles out to sea before they found her body. There was the little Chinese girl in Hong Kong and the chatty little redhead in Liverpool, and...

He had to give them "Lara's Theme" several times and when they left there were back-slappings and "Good old Pete's."

"That was wonderful, Pete," said his mother as they drove home. "You're a good boy."

At about the time Anders was returning to Forebridge and Mellish was playing the piano, Harry Bristow and Tom Purdy were having a quiet drink together in the saloon bar of the Red Lion.

A few convivial spirits at the other end of the bar were enjoying a joke at the expense of one of their party, and a rotund gentleman in a tweed suit was almost beside himself with mirth as he rolled against the bar counter.

But neither Bristow nor Purdy felt like laughing. Joe Murray was their friend. He was sincere and open and yet self-contained, a man who shared but kept part of himself aloof. The terrible shadow which was cast over him touched Purdy and Bristow as well. They had both been with the searchers until the early hours of the morning and then, after a wash and shave, had been obliged to catch up again with the daily pattern.

They had both heard of the abduction of Peggy Finney.

Bristow lowered his glass and wiped some froth from his mouth with the back of his hand. "Not much doubt about it now. I can't understand how anyone..." He shook his head in disgust. "I mean why? Going round tracking down little kids! And what are the bloody police doing?"

"I don't know," said Purdy, "but it can't be easy. Say you had the job, where would you start?"

"It's not my job. I'm not trained for it and I'm not paid for it."

"But just think about it! What have you got to go on? The only witnesses are dead, poor little devils. You're looking for

50

a cunning bastard with a car, and it's not like an ordinary crime with some motive behind it. He could be anybody."

"Joe'll never get over it, you know. Never knew a chap so keen on children. I remember him once going all serious about it—it was before they'd had Angela. We'd been having a chat at my place and, jokingly, I happened to mention I thought he was a lucky bugger—strong as an ox, comfortably off, happy home life and so on—when he went to the window and stared at my kids playing in the garden. 'Except for one thing,' he said. 'I'd trade in most of what I've got if we could have a child of our own.' He went on a bit more but it was the expression on his face that hit me."

Purdy shook his head sadly and they both sat silently sipping their beer.

"All the time everybody's wondering when the bastard's going to strike next," said Purdy. "And what can you do?"

"Nothing except what we *are* doing—taking each other's kids to school, never letting them out of our sight. We can't keep that up for ever."

"I hear the police have been round the schools giving advice."

"Bit late for that," said Bristow sourly. He gazed thoughtfully into his glass. "Funny thing! If it hadn't been for this business, my wife and I would have had it."

"How come?"

"I was just walking out. Got my cases all ready to put in the car. There we were, neither of us willing to give in, and I was actually about to open the door for the last time when you rang."

"Your wife answered the phone."

"That's right. She was standing in the hall. It had been coming for months. Anyway, I dropped everything, as you know, and when I got back I was too damn tired to think about it and she'd sort of changed, so it seemed pointless. I reckon too we both thought that it could have been one of our kids."

"Interesting," said Purdy, "and odd as well," and he was

tempted. He'd meant it when he promised Stringer not to say anything. But confidences beget confidences and Bristow would, after all, keep it to himself. "You know Mavis Stringer?"

"Of course I do. You know I do."

"What d'you reckon to her?"

"She's got some chassis, I know that. And behind that haughty act I'd say she could be a hot cookie and doesn't get enough. And I wouldn't mind obliging her if I could be sure she'd keep her mouth shut."

"On the night we were searching, someone did oblige her. This won't go any further, will it?"

"No. No, of course not."

"George was with me in my car. Mavis had his. We went down to the old quarry and, would you bloody well believe it, there was his car behind a bush and in the back, half stripped, was Mavis performing with some bloke!"

"Christ! What did George do?"

"Nothing. Staggered off and looked as if he was going to pass out. Wouldn't get back in the car either. Asked me not to say anything. But hearing about your business, I thought it a bit ironic—other way round, as it were. And I know you'll keep it under your hat."

"Who was the man?"

"Haven't the faintest. Only saw the back of his head and his shoulders."

George Stringer was asking his wife the same question. "Who is he?"

They were the first words he'd uttered to her since the previous evening. He had gone to bed but sleep had been impossible, and he had left for the office earlier than usual, hoping that some order would come to the wreckage of his confused mind.

As a manager of a reputable finance firm and an employee of long standing, he would have needed no excuses if he had absented himself. Perhaps it would have been better if he had done so, for the passing hours had been torture and he had been unable to concentrate.

Coming home in the train he had decided that the issue had to be faced squarely and that it was no good burying his head in the sand. Things like this only happened to other people and he had been firmly convinced that, if ever he were on the receiving end, that would be that! Finish, and no second chance. Soiled goods could never be for him.

But reality brought a different reaction. He found that he still loved her and, as if to a life line, he clung to the hope that it was only a passing affair, that she had given way during a period of emotional imbalance.

He went in the back way and as he passed through the kitchen the smell of cooking and the warmth from the oven lifted him slightly. At least she was still behaving normally in this respect.

She was in the sitting-room, staring out of the window, and he stood in the doorway for a few moments. Then, moving to the window a few feet from her, he also stared out as he put the question. "Who is he?"

"Nobody you know."

"How long?" he asked and, when she didn't answer, he said: "Do you love him?"

"Yes."

The kick in the stomach returned. "But why? What have I done?"

Out of the corner of his eye he could see her glance at him. "Nothing. It's just the way it happened. I didn't mean it to."

"Can't you stop seeing him?"

"I told you; I love him."

He swallowed the bile which had come to his throat. "What does that mean? You want to go with him . . . leave here?"

"I think so. Yes. I can't . . . not see him. And I can't stop here now."

He turned towards her, his face strained with emotion. "Wait! See him if you must. I can't very well stop you if you feel like that. But don't go until you're sure. Something could happen—you might need me."

"You're trying to make me feel sorry for you. I can't help it. I didn't do it to hurt you."

"I understand that. And being sorry for me won't help. All I ask is—wait."

"Who was with you?"

"Only Tom Purdy and he's promised not to say anything. Nobody else need know if it all fizzles out."

She glanced at him again and then went to the door. "I'll get dinner. Then I'm going out. I won't take the car, and I'll do something about getting one of my own tomorrow."

CHAPTER 5

The next morning the photokit picture appeared in the newspapers. HAVE YOU SEEN THIS MAN? There was a description of the man who was wanted for the abduction of a girl of seven in Forebridge and a description of the car, giving the colour, type, possible make and the fact that the number was believed to contain an 'H' and a three. There was also an urgent plea for anyone having any information to contact the police immediately.

At first Mellish stiffened, like a fox which has scented the hounds. Then, after studying it carefully, he came to the conclusion he hadn't anything to worry about. They hadn't got the car number and the picture, although not a bad likeness, was obviously only a guide. It could equally apply to hundreds of other men of about his age. Fortunately he had worn the blue shirt and slacks only that once and he doubted if his mother would have noticed what colour they were.

When she came in, he pushed over the paper and pointed to the item. "Look at that, Ma. Pictures of a man wanted about that girl."

She stopped by the table and peered at the paper. "Ooh!"

she said. "It's something like your Uncle Charlie, only he was dead before you were born."

He put out a hand as she started to move off again. "You'd better read the description in case you see him out somewhere."

"Fancy that," she said and went into the kitchen.

At ten o'clock he rang Mavis Stringer and immediately expressed concern for her. "I've been thinking about you all the time and wondering if you were all right."

"Last night he asked me who you were."

"Did you tell him?"

"No. I told him that I loved you. He thinks I'll get over it."

"Will you?"

"Do you want me to?"

"You shouldn't ask questions like that. I want to see you all the time. When can you make it?"

"I'm going to buy a car. I can't use his any more. I can't."

He turned this over in his mind. Not a bad idea, but it mustn't be anything like the last one. "Have you got anybody to help you?" he asked.

"No. I thought about going to one of those places in Broad Street."

"How much are you thinking of paying?"

"Four hundred—will that do?"

"Not if you go on your own. They'll fleece you. Leave it to me. What sort of car do you want?"

"I don't mind as long as it's respectable and no trouble."

"Can I pick you up somewhere, say at two o'clock?"

"Outside Boots, I've got to go there."

"Right. Bring the cash with you. These chaps don't like cheques."

There were two places he considered going to. Frankie Hay's Car Mart and Sullivan's. He knew Frankie Hay personally but he thought Lenny Myall at Sullivan's would bend easier, so he went there. A gunmetal, stand-up Renault caught his eye and he looked round it. It didn't seem in bad shape, hardly any rust and the tyres were reasonable. It was taxed to the end of the year and was marked up for three-seventy-five.

"What's it like?" he asked Lenny Myall.

Myall screwed up his leathery face and gazed at the car affectionately.

"Good buy. I won't give you the usual spiel. Try her."

Mellish tried her and when he brought the car back he said: "I'll give you two-seventy."

"Come off it!"

"All right. Name a reasonable price."

"Three-fifty?"

"Three-twenty-five."

"OK, OK. But it's rock bottom. Bloody robbery."

"I want it for a client of mine, a woman I've done a couple of jobs for. Mark it up for four hundred pounds, take three hundred and seventy-five and give me the fifty when the deal's done."

Myall glanced at him sideways. "Ain't no grass growing on you! OK. When?"

"This afternoon, two-fifteen to two-thirty."

"I can't hold it if someone else wants it before then."

Mellish felt in his back pocket and produced two five-pound notes. "That do? You owe me sixty."

"OK. I'll hold it."

Mavis Stringer put on a new, white, sleeveless dress which finished just above her knees. She was forty-one and her figure, as with some women of her age, was in its prime. A little extra care with her make-up removed at least ten years from her face.

Mentally she was in a state of suspension, sometimes riding high on a cloud of euphoria and sometimes looking down at the conscience which beckoned her. But she would always shut her eyes and ears to conscience and dwell on thoughts which helped to justify her behaviour. Was it her fault that George was inadequate, content in only occasionally satisfying himself, subsiding into a deep sleep after a few, brief and clumsy caresses and a sudden bout of agitation? For years she had endured it, until she was on the point of accepting that there was anything more to it and that women were only the vehicle with which men relieved their tensions and appetites.

But how wrong she would have been. Peter had shown her. It was out of this world. And it wasn't her fault; it wasn't her fault that George couldn't be like Peter or that she hadn't met Peter first.

Now and again a picture of George came to her, as he had stood near her at the window. "Wait!" he had said. "You may need me." But she had put it from her as she did any doubts about Peter and how long it would last.

He was waiting for her and when she got in beside him and he looked at her, the swift, burning sensation which she usually experienced when she first met him ran up from the pit of her stomach.

She wasn't very impressed with the look of the car he showed her. She would have preferred a different shape and colour. But she trusted him and was pleased that he'd been able to knock twenty-five pounds off the price. She felt the salesman undressing her with his eyes, but she didn't notice the half-amused look on his face as he glanced from one to the other. She paid the money and collected the log book, together with a cover note from the firm who were also agents for an insurance company, and then she took possession of the car.

Mellish left his Mini in a corner out of the way and drove the Renault for her until they reached a quiet stretch of road, when she took over. In a short time she was agreeably surprised at the way the car handled and she soon familiarized herself with the controls. "You're quite an expert," he said. "Not many people could get in a strange car and drive it like this."

"I've always liked driving. My brother taught me. He was a police driver."

He looked the other way for a moment. "Well, he did a good job on you. D'you still see him?"

"No. That was a long time ago. He's in Canada."

"In the police?"

"Yes. I think he'll be retiring shortly. I hear from him about once a year."

"I haven't thought of asking before, but have you anybody else, a mother, father or anybody who'd be upset about us?"

"No, only him. Both my parents died years ago. What about you?"

He gave a short laugh. "Nobody's ever worried about me—except you. The only thing that'll worry my mother is that she might not get enough for her bingo. My father was in the Merchant Navy and died when I was six. Fell overboard, so I've been told."

She felt for his hand.

"How long have we got?" he asked.

"Hours. I'm not bothering about when I get back."

"Turn left at the next junction and head for Pawleigh."

"That's a long way."

"Only about twenty-five miles. I'm supposed to be doing a plastering job any day this week for a man who's got a weekend bungalow there. He's told me where to find the key so I can get in."

"There won't be anybody there?"

"No. That's why he told me where to find the key."

It was true that he knew where to find the key and, allowing for the extreme unlikelihood of the owner returning from London in mid-week, it was true that there would be nobody there. But he had finished the plastering over a month ago and he knew where to find the key because the owner hadn't been careful enough when he had collected it from its rather obvious hiding-place.

"What's it like?" she asked.

"It's got four rooms and a bathroom and kitchen, and it's white stucco with a verandah. You get to it by going down an unmade road and it has a hedge one side and wattle fencing on the other side and at the back. There's also a hedge in the front and behind it is a river. No one'll see us, so you needn't worry about that."

The warning note of a police siren intruded and grew louder. Masking the wariness which instantly commanded his senses, he turned casually and looked through the rear window. They were two hundred yards away and coming fast.

"Keep over," he said. "They're on a call somewhere."

Another burst on the siren before they swept past, and then he relaxed in his seat again, enjoying the smug satisfaction he felt when he thought that only he knew! Out of everybody in the whole world only he knew and that was how it would always be because he was far too clever for them.

It was just as he had said. He directed her down the concealed turning and in seconds they were hidden from the main road. The slightly bumpy but firm track wound in a series of bends through hedges for a hundred yards, and then they came to a wide, slatted gate which he opened for her and shut again when she had driven through. At his suggestion she parked behind the detached wooden garage.

He took her hand as they walked across to the bungalow and the anticipation of what was to come sent the blood to her temples and her pulses racing. She forced her voice to keep calm. "Is it nice inside?"

"You'll see," he said and, feeling behind one of the verandah beams, produced the key.

It was carpeted throughout—a delicate shade of blue, except for the kitchen which she half noticed as they passed it.

Then they were in the bedroom and all she was conscious of was pale pink walls, a low, wide bed—and Peter Mellish. He didn't rush at it. How different he was! He kissed her and his hands slid over her. The buttons of her dress he slipped over without fumbling and his mouth, with darting tongue, found her neck and shoulders as he pulled back her dress. She was floating in a glorious dream. It could have taken seconds or hours. She was naked and he was naked and he was holding her and kissing her in that particular way he had: her breasts, her back, her arms and then down until she gasped and almost wanted to scream in ecstasy.

And then, with perfect timing, he eased his attentions as they relaxed on the bed. She felt for him and found him, hard and virile, and for a while she changed the roles. Suddenly he held her fiercely and forced her back, hurting her, and then he entered her.

He came again, three times before they left, and only then was she completely satisfied.

On the journey back he talked lightly and hopefully mentioned the job in Newcastle. "There is one thing," he said. "I hadn't thought of it before. Frank is rather old-fashioned and if he knew about us it might make him kick. You're sure nobody knows about me?"

"Nobody knows who you are."

"Good! Keep it that way and when we go you can be Mrs. Mellish. They won't know where you've come from."

By the morning of the 6th June, the team of detectives who had been detailed to check the motor taxation files had recorded 1,459 olive green or dark green saloon cars with a permutation of numbers containing an "H" and a three. They included 261 Austin 1800s and 1,198 similar type models of other makes.

The preliminary list went to the Forebridge Murder Headquarters and at ten o'clock fifteen pairs of detectives departed with questionnaire forms to check on the owners. This team was superimposed on the team of thirty pairs of detectives engaged on the mammoth task of interviewing every householder and every male over sixteen in the district.

And the search for Angela Murray continued. So far, apart from the shoe found earlier, there had been no trace of her. For hour after hour lines of police, soldiers and civilians, shoulder to shoulder, had combed every inch of the surrounding area. Occasionally there had been replacements but most of them had stayed the course. Inaccessible and unlikely places had been explored by highly-trained police dogs and every building had been checked by a team of fifty uniformed policemen who had been left in no doubt what would happen to them if the girl were subsequently found on the patches allocated to them.

Inevitably there were side effects. Frogmen fished out from the river nine rusty bicycles and several items of interest, including a cunningly-concealed waterproof metal box which was found to contain nearly fifty thousand pounds, the proceeds of a seven-year-old robbery. The culprit, at present in Pentonville, was due out on parole at any moment.

By mid-day the posters had been printed and a picture of Angela, with her description, was fixed on all public noticeboards and others in the district. An hour later another picture went up and was placed alongside that of the girl. It was a blown-up reproduction of the photokit likeness of "The Predator," as he had come to be known, which had already appeared in the newspapers and on television. Copies were sent to every police force in the country.

All thought of normal leave was out of the question. There were a few disgruntled ones but a number of officers voluntarily cancelled their holidays.

On the 8th June, Anders paid a brief visit to his home and, after a bath and change of clothing, returned with enough personal equipment to see him through another week. The slightly unreal feeling induced by prolonged lack of sleep was with him but he had got his second wind. This was how it would be with them all—snatches of rest, an hour here and there, as long as they could stand it.

The Murder Headquarters had again been reorganized. Filing cases and indexes accommodated the mass of paper work which was accumulating. This was the main hope. Every scrap of information on every scrap of paper had to be treated with respect, itemized, classified and indexed so that relevant items could be extracted and added to any pattern which might appear to be forming. There were no short cuts. Miss one small, apparently insignificant point, and they might well draw irretrievably further and further away from their goal.

Chief Superintendent Jordan from Coolidge paid them a visit and Anders looked at his grey face with concern. The man looked ill. He was alert enough and obviously as efficient as ever, but he was fighting something and there were tell-tale signs: the yellow flecks in the white of his eyes and the pallor of his skin.

At his suggestion, arrangements were made to fix a close-circuit television link between the two headquarters so that no time would be wasted in comparing documents or inspecting visual clues which might come to light.

At 6:45 p.m. on the same day, two detective-constables walked up the front path of 27 Drayton Road. As always, they took in the aspect of the place, noting its air of affluence and the small grey Renault parked on the driveway in front of the garage.

When Mavis Stringer opened the door they took her in also and, being normal healthy animals, they classified her, if only fleetingly, as a promising, bedworthy companion.

Mavis Stringer saw two young men who had that slight touch of arrogant self-assurance which seemed to put them in some official bracket or other. The one with fair hair and pale blue eyes said: "Mrs. Stringer?"

"Yes?"

He produced a police warrant card. "According to Taxation, Mrs. Stringer, a green Austin 1800, number HGO 434J, is owned by a Mr. George William Stringer who lives here."

"Yes. It belongs to my husband. It's in the garage."

"We're on a routine investigation to do with the abduction of a small child on the 5th June and also the murder of several children in Coolidge over the past six months. We have a questionnaire we'd like your husband's co-operation in filling in."

"Murder? Children? Surely you don't think my husband . . . ?"

He drew a deep breath. Same old routine! Same old flannel!

"Of course not, madam. Every owner of a green Austin has to be seen. It's all part of the elimination process."

"I see. Well, he's not home yet."

"When will he be home?"

"Could be any time now. I'm expecting him."

"Do you mind if we come in? Perhaps you can provide some of the answers while we're waiting."

"All right." She stood aside for them, shut the door and led them into the sitting-room. They behaved casually but their eyes were everywhere. After a nod of assent from her, they both followed her example and sat down.

"I see by the records that your husband has owned the car for nearly two years. Who drives it?"

"Me mostly. My husband does sometimes."

"Nobody else?"

"No. There's nobody else here."

"Would you mind letting me have your full name?"

"Mavis Eileen Stringer."

"Can you tell me who was driving it yesterday at about three-thirty p.m.?"

"Yes. I was."

"Where was your husband at the time?"

"He was at his office in town, of course."

"I'm sorry but this is all necessary and it will save us calling again. We're doing it with everybody. Where does he work and what does he do for a living?"

The officer saw the suddenly-compressed lips and added: "You do know about the child murders at Coolidge?"

"Of course I do. It's dreadful, absolutely dreadful."

"And that a child of nine has been missing from Forebridge since Monday?"

"Yes, I know about that."

"You'll appreciate then that we've got to ask personal questions of everybody. But it's all treated as confidential."

She shrugged. "It doesn't matter but I can't see what his job's got to do with it. I don't suppose *he'll* mind. He's a manager for a finance firm, Marlow and Brook of Cannon Street in the City."

He waited for his colleague to finish scribbling. "Where did you go at three-thirty yesterday?"

"To my dressmaker in Milton Avenue."

"Were you there for long?"

"About an hour."

"Was anybody else with you?"

"No. My dressmaker will confirm it. She lives at number 15."

"I don't know whether you can help here," said the officer, referring to the form, "but do these dates mean anything to you? The 9th January, 23rd February and 6th April? Can you say where the car was on the afternoon of those dates?"

"What days of the week would they be?"

"Strangely enough, they're all Fridays."

"I would have been at the hairdresser's then. I have a regular appointment and I didn't miss any."

"At about what time?"

"I go there every Friday at half past three."

"Where is your hairdresser?"

"Jacques in Byfleet."

He smiled at her. "It's very good of you to be so cooperative, Mrs. Stringer. The quicker we can eliminate people, the sooner we'll get somewhere. Whose is the Renault outside, by the way?"

"It's mine."

"So you have two cars in the family, but on Tuesday you used your husband's instead of your own?"

"I didn't get mine until Wednesday."

"I see."

There was the sound of movement from the hall and the front door shut quietly.

"That'll be my husband," she said and, as she stood up, they got to their feet, both sensing a trace of uneasiness in her manner, and when a middle-aged, rather ordinary-looking man came into the room, she didn't seem anxious to look at him.

The officers filed away a picture of him: five-feet, eight inches, forty-five to fifty, slim build, slight paunch, brown hair receding and balding on top, nose rather prominent, lines round wide mouth, mild expression on face, wearing well-cut grey suit, black shoes, white shirt and red, blue and gold striped tie. His arched eyebrows were raised in surprise and, as she wasn't offering an explanation, they introduced themselves and told him the reason for their visit.

Stringer nodded as if he were thinking of something else. "Yes. I went on the first search party for the Murray child." His quick glance at his wife didn't go undetected. "Murray's a friend of mine. I suppose there's no news?"

"I'm afraid not, sir. But we have a description of the man we want to interview."

"Yes. I've seen the photographs."

"Your wife has kindly given what information she can. Would you mind checking through the questionnaire we've filled in, to see if you agree with it and if there's anything you can add?"

"On the dates mentioned you were in London, in your office?"

"Yes. I've no objection if you want to check with my firm."

"I doubt if we'll need to do that, sir, but there is one thing. We'd like to have a look at the car."

"Certainly. We'll go into the garage by the back way."

Mrs. Stringer had quietly left the room.

Outside in the car again, the officer who had been compiling the questionnaire added his conclusions to the form: "Wife physically attractive, husband ordinary. Seems some tension between them. Wife normally drives car and has free use of it but on 6th June she bought car of her own, a grey Renault LEG 561G. Mr. Stringer no likeness to suspect."

CHAPTER 6

At 3:15 P.M. on the 13th June, another pair of constables called at 113 Cluny Avenue, one of a group of semidetached yellow-brick council houses with short front lawns and no boundary fences.

Mrs. Mellish, who opened the door, took the cigarette out of her mouth and peered at them suspiciously through a thin stream of curling smoke. They explained the purpose of their visit and immediately decided that here was another case which called for a resolute approach.

She sniffed and shook her head. "About the kid, is it? I can't help you. We've got no murderers living here."

"I hope not, but that's for us to decide. If you don't mind, we'll come inside."

There was a moment's hesitation and then she led them into a front room. It had a green fitted carpet, an ugly three-piece suite, grey and pink striped wallpaper and woodwork painted an odd shade of mushroom. A twenty-two-inch television set dominated one corner.

"Who lives here?"

"Me and my boy."

"And you're Mrs. . . . ?"

"Mellish."

"Christian names?"

"Pris."

"Pris?"

"Priscilla."

"Any others?"

"Susan, but they all call me Pris."

"Your son, how old is he?"

She had to work this out. "Thirty-six."

"His name?"

"Pete."

"D'you mean Peter?"

"Yes, that's right, Peter."

"He's not married?"

"No."

"This is his permanent address?"

"It's his home whenever he likes."

"He's not here all the time then?"

"He's been about a bit. Seen the world, he has, like his
father."

The officer's pen moved a trifle more slowly over the paper.

"Where is his father?"

"Been dead over twenty years."

"How long has your son lived here with you?"

She closed one eye at a hideous china clock on the mantelpiece. "About nine months since the last time."

"How d'you mean, the last time?"

"I told you. He travels about. In the Merchant Navy once."

"What does he do for a living?"

"Anything."

"That's not quite good enough, Mrs. Mellish. Has he got
a trade?"

"He can do anything: carpentry, bricking, electrics, plastering. He's very clever is my Pete."

The officers glanced at each other and a further entry was
made.

"Who does he work for?"

"All sorts of people, builders and anyone who recommends him."

"He really works for himself then?"

"I suppose he does."

"And he doesn't work regular hours?"

"Not really. Here, what is this? What's he done? My Pete's no murderer."

They read the signs: without a little soft soap now she'd shut up like a clam. "I'm sure he isn't. Don't get upset. These questions are being asked of everybody."

"I can't see..."

"Look here! Suppose your Pete was murdered, you'd expect us to do something about it, wouldn't you?"

"Yes, well..."

"And if we knew a man was responsible, we'd have to see a lot of innocent men before we came to the right one. It's not easy, you know. Now, let's try and eliminate your Pete from being a suspect, shall we? It's quite easy. Where were you last Tuesday afternoon?"

"Me? I went to the Palace."

"The Palace?"

"Bingo hall, used to be a cinema."

"What time did you leave here?"

"About half past one and got back just before six."

"Where was your son all this time?"

"He was at home."

"On his own?"

"As far as I know."

"He hadn't any job to do for anybody?"

"He was working on his car."

"So you left him about one-thirty and didn't see him anymore until nearly six?"

"Yes, I suppose so."

"That's fine, Mrs. Mellish. I wish everybody was as helpful and frank as you are. What car does he drive, by the way?"

"He can drive anything, can Pete."

"Yes, but what sort does he own, or does he?"

"He's got a Mini with a door at the back so he can put his stuff in."

The officer asking the questions nodded affably while he thought about it. "He drives other cars sometimes, does he?"

"When anybody asks him. I don't know too much about what he does."

"Any particular car you can remember?"

She shrugged and lit another cigarette. "Got no idea. Sometimes he says somebody or other wants him to drive their car somewhere but I never see it and it's not very often. I don't think he likes that much. Prefers working with his hands."

"When will he be home?"

"Can't say for sure. Shouldn't think before six."

"We'll come back about half past six and then we won't bother you any more. We've been instructed to see everybody and they'll be bound to check on us."

"Oh, all right," she said and followed them to the door. "Supposing he doesn't come back until later?"

"We'll have to keep calling until we *do* see him. Thank you, Mrs. Mellish."

But it was nearer five when Mellish returned home, feeling fairly pleased with himself. He had finished a room conversion, knocking down a wall and providing a shallow arch in its place. It was a beautiful job, especially the plastering and final touches, and the owner had been so pleased with it that he paid ten pounds over the asking price.

He washed and removed some of his five o'clock shadow with his electric razor and changed into a fawn shirt and brown suit which he brushed meticulously. Then he combed his eyebrows and moved his face close to the mirror, baring his strong, white teeth in a brief examination. He was on the point of leaving when he took the small portable mirror from its shelf and focused it so that he could see his profile and side view in the larger mirror over the dressing-table. Satisfied, he went down.

His mother, who had been gossiping over the fence with

the woman next door, came in as he put on the kettle to make some tea. "Oh," he said, "you're home!"

"My, you do look smart, Pete! Going somewhere special?"

"Navy and Military for a start. I'm in the finals of the snooker tournament."

"I expect you'll win."

"Maybe. Should do. After that, I'm going to the Anniversary Club. Got a bit of a 'do' on there."

"Can I come?"

"No, you bloody well can't." He felt in his pocket and, pulling out a few notes, extracted a fiver and threw it on the table. "That's something to keep you going tomorrow."

She scooped it up. "Thanks, Pete. Sit down and I'll get you something." A few minutes later she called out from the kitchen: "The police came this afternoon."

For a moment he froze, and then he sauntered out to join her. "What did *they* want?"

"They're going round to everybody, about this girl missing and the murders."

"What did you tell them?"

"They wanted to know who was living here and what we did, and what you were doing last Tuesday afternoon."

"Tuesday afternoon? I've forgotten what I was doing."

"I told them you were doing a job on your car here."

"Oh yes, I'm glad you remembered. Anything else?"

"Usual nosy questions coppers ask. They're coming back about half past six to see you. Said they had to see everyone."

"They'll be lucky! I shan't be here."

"They'll only come again. They said so. May as well get it over with, Pete."

"Yes," he said thoughtfully. "Perhaps you're right. But if they're not here on time, I'm going and I can't spare them long anyway."

But as he said it, there was a ring at the doorbell. The detectives had had second thoughts about Mellish and, driving past earlier than they had arranged, they had seen the Mini parked outside the house.

71

Mrs. Mellish opened the door and Mellish nodded at them as they came in.

They had already decided that they had enough information, but they wanted a look at him. Against every man they hadn't seen there remained a question mark and, from what his mother had unwittingly let pass, this was another one with possibilities.

"Thought we would call a bit earlier in case you wanted to go out."

Mellish gave them his usual enigmatic stare. "Glad you did. I've got an appointment at seven. It's about this kid, I understand?"

"That's right. You don't mind?"

"Why should I? You've got your job to do."

"Just a few points. Will you confirm where you were and what you were doing last Tuesday afternoon?"

"I was here, changing the cylinder head gasket on my car."

"All the afternoon? Say from two until five?"

"Yes. I was here."

"You didn't go anywhere else?"

"I strolled down to the shops for some cigarettes," said Mellish, remembering that he had in fact done so before he went out. The confirmation, he thought, added a nice touch.

"One other point. Do you ever drive a green car?"

Mellish flinched inside as the dart hit the outer ring but he showed nothing. "I can't remember. I may have done but not recently."

"I see. Well, that seems all right. No point in bothering you further."

"You've got a hell of a job on."

"You can say that again. Good evening, then, Mr. Mellish—Mrs. Mellish."

Before the officers drove away, final comments were added to the form: "Peter Mellish: some likeness to photo-picture, description tallies. No actual corroboration yet of movements on afternoon of Tuesday, 5th June. Worth further attention."

CHAPTER 7

By the end of the second week, the searchers had covered over four thousand acres, nine thousand houses had been visited and nearly thirty thousand persons accounted for. Anders, at the end of each analysis and searching every sheet hopefully for even one small sign to point them in the right direction, realized how frustrating it must have been and still was for Jordan, who had been doing this for month after month.

At midnight on the Friday, a row of selected officers were still at a long table carefully checking the questionnaires. Anything doubtful was noted and the form put in a separate file which was collected regularly and taken to another long table for further examination.

The officer who came to the Stringer form pondered on it for a while and then got up and took it to Detective Chief Inspector Carver for further guidance. "On the face of it, sir, there's nothing in this one but I think the remarks are worth noting."

"Hmm!" said Carver as he glanced at it. "She bought a car for herself the day after the abduction. Nothing much in that."

"It mentions the air of tension between Mr. and Mrs.

Stringer and, although *he's* been ruled out, it says that she's had almost exclusive use of his car."

Carver read it through again. "All right," he said, "there's probably nothing in it but mark it and put it with others to be dealt with tomorrow."

Because of his local knowledge, Sergeant Gisling had been transferred into plain clothes and seconded to the murder team, and the following morning he was given the Stringer enquiry, with instructions to work cautiously from the outside.

His first port of call was the Motor Taxation Office to trace the previous owner of the grey Renault, and at ten o'clock he descended on Sullivan Car Sales, to be greeted by Lenny Myall.

With laconic good humour, Myall said: "Hallo, Bill! Come to buy a decent car at last?"

"Why, do you sell 'em? No, Lenny, this is police business." Gisling produced his notebook. "The other day you sold a grey Renault number LEG 561G?"

Myall pursed his lips. "I'll just check the number and the details." He led Gisling to a small glass office at the side where he sorted through an untidy collection of papers before he found what he wanted. "Sold it to a dame." He grinned. "Here we are: Mrs. Mavis Stringer of 27 Drayton Road." Then he chuckled.

"What's so funny?"

Myall chuckled again. "Some bloke I know did all right. Knocked me down on the price and then got me to mark it up before he brought her along to buy it. Made fifty quid for himself."

Gisling rolled a cigarette and lit it, and then got out his notebook again. "What time of day was this?"

"He came in the morning. Brought her in the afternoon. If you want a good bet, he's shagging her and I reckon she'd be worth it too, lucky bugger."

"You say you know this bloke."

"Sort of. I only know him as Pete. Don't know his surname or where he lives."

"What's he like to look at?"

"About as tall as you but not so broad in the beam. Dark, not bad looking."

"What was he wearing?"

Myall shook his head and frowned. "Now you've got me. Dark shirt and trousers, I think—probably brown. But don't stick to that. If you told me he had a green shirt, I wouldn't argue."

"D'you know anything about him?"

"Nothing much. He's fly. If he tried to sell me anything, I'd want its pedigree."

"What does he do for a living?"

"Something in the building line, I think."

"He's got a car?"

"At the moment he's driving a red Mini Estate."

"Thanks, Lenny." Gisling shut his book and put it away.

"What's it about? She done a hit and run?"

"No. It's probably nothing."

"Why you interested in him then?"

"I'm interested in everybody—even you!"

Gisling reported back with his information at 11:15 a.m. and by 11:20 Carver had extracted from the system all the files of men named Peter. There were fifty-nine and a little research whittled the number down to five. These he took to Anders. "Gisling has come up with something," he said, and slid the report on to the Superintendent's table.

"Have you sorted anybody out?" said Anders.

"Eight possibles, but a chap named Mellish looks the most promising. Here's his file. The description fits, he's got a red Mini Estate and there's no corroboration so far where he was on Tuesday afternoon."

Anders read it through carefully and then went back, making a pencil ring around each point of note. Eventually he handed it back to Carver. "He sounds a bright boy. Put a tail on him and get someone to check his engine without his knowing it. And for the time being, keep away from Mrs. Stringer."

"Right. It's a relief to get at least a nibble. There's not much in the others but I'll have them checked again."

At 2 a.m. on Monday, 18th June, a grey saloon car, with its engine shut off, coasted along Cluny Avenue and came to a halt in one of the few vacant spaces near Mellish's Mini. Two figures got out and one of them with a bunch of keys eventually opened the driver's door. Then he lifted the bonnet and the other shone a torch on to the engine. After a brief examination they shut it quietly, locked the car door and drove off. Of one thing they were certain: the cylinder head hadn't been removed for a long time.

At 9 o'clock Mellish came out of the house, threw a few tools into the back of the Mini and, through a hole in a Post Office van, a camera clicked. Mellish drove off and a battered Ford Consul, with a boiler-suited, long-haired young man driving, followed.

After a mile Mellish stopped at a builders' merchants and strolled inside. Behind the long wooden counter, the jaded-looking individual in a fawn dustcoat gave a sign of recognition. Mellish said: "Morning, Harry. Ballcock and valve, new type, plastic."

The assistant disappeared and after a few minutes returned with the necessary equipment. The boiler-suited Ford driver waited patiently in the background. Mellish examined the goods. "That's OK. I want some filling compound as well. Thompson's, if you've got it."

The assistant moved to a shelf, reached up and produced a large round tin.

"That's it," said Mellish. "What's the damage?"

There was a brief reference to the price list, some scribbling on a pad and the assistant tore off the top sheet and handed it over. Mellish paid and the assistant gave him his change and said: "Who're you playing in the final?"

"Harold Pierce."

"You won't have a tighter game than the last one. How you

got out of that bloody snooker at the end beats me. That's what decided it."

Mellish collected his purchases. "You coming on Friday?"

"Might do. What time is it?"

"Eight, at the Union not the Club."

"Why's that?"

"Doing some repairs there. Anyway, might see you!"

"Ta-ra, Pete."

Mellish raised his free hand and disappeared.

The assistant condescendingly turned his attention to the man in the boiler suit, who suddenly clapped his hand to his breast pocket and exclaimed: "Damn! I've left my wallet behind. I'll be back."

All that day the air had become increasingly oppressive and just before midnight the storm broke: great choking claps of thunder followed by angry rumbles and rain that thudded earthwards as if it meant to go on for ever.

But Mellish, sitting up in bed, immobile, seemed oblivious of it all. The curtains were drawn back and occasionally lightning streaked across the sky, spotlighting the silver blobs of rain which hurried down the window, and flashing a fierce glare through the room and over Mellish's impassive features.

He had come to a decision. Mavis Stringer had begun to bore him; she was an irritation. The only satisfaction she could give him now would be to see her with her eyes bulging, gaping and choking her life away after he had taken her.

But there was more to it than that. She was a danger. Even if he continued to play along for a while, the time would come, not far off, when he would have to end it. She'd reached the stage when she could no longer take it or leave it. And what might she do? The police were looking for a green saloon. Supposing she told them that he had driven hers? And told them, moreover, that he had driven it at certain specific times on certain specific dates? As things were at present between them, he knew that she would go to the stake rather than implicate him. No one connected him personally with her or the car and, although her husband had seen him, he wouldn't be able to recognize him again. And he didn't know he'd driven the car. If she were eliminated, there would be no one to bear witness against him, no one!

Having decided on the fact, he began to work out the means. It would have to look natural. He was lucky there. She had just bought a car, a second-hand car. A mechanical defect? Yes, but nothing obvious, no broken parts to give the game away. The brake fluid? Master cylinder? How simple! She wasn't a bad driver but knew nothing, absolutely nothing, about the mechanism. "Something not quite right there," he could say and while she sat inside he could lift the bonnet, uncover the cap from the master cylinder and suck out the fluid with a hose and ball. She wouldn't see a thing.

What then? It would have to be final. He knew just the place. Hanbury bridge, up by the gorge, with a drop of at least a hundred feet and the river below. She'd plough right through the fence. Easy! It was an isolated place and a fair way off, about forty miles. But she wouldn't mind that and it would take them less than a couple of hours. He was seeing her at seven. They'd be there well before nine. Afterwards he could walk to Pullford and get a train.

That was it then! He'd polish off the details later but to-morrow it would have to be. Tomorrow? No, today!

With a feeling of satisfaction in his own astuteness and invulnerability, he slid down the sheets and went to sleep.

CHAPTER 8

In the morning the sun shone again. The streets of Forebridge, washed by the heavy persistent rain, looked clean and wholesome and a damp, invigorating fragrance from the trees and gardens filled the air. Lenny Myall, whistling tunelessly but cheerfully, was opening his office door when he realized that Sergeant Gisling was standing by one of the cars on the lot, watching him.

"Morning, Lenny," said Gisling. "Nice to see you so happy first thing."

"What's up now?"

Gisling thrust a photograph in front of him. "Is that him?"

Myall examined it and nodded slowly. "That's him, yes."

"The man Pete?"

"Yes. Here, there's more in this. Am I going to get involved in something?"

"Not if you keep your mouth shut. And if you don't I'll invoke the Gisling Law!"

Myall looked after Gisling as he went to his car. "I've heard about that," he said.

By 3 p.m. at Murder Headquarters a definite pattern had emerged and had been checked and confirmed.

1. Peggy Finney abducted on 5th June.
2. Photo-kit picture accepted by two children at Coolidge.
3. Wanted man believed local, pronounced Sethley as Selly.
4. Suspect car believed to be olive green Austin 1800 or similar.
5. Number contained an 'H' and a three.
6. Car owned by Mr. Stringer qualified.
7. Mr. Stringer ruled out as suspect.
8. Car used mainly by Mrs. Stringer.
9. On day of abduction, she drove it to her dressmaker in Forebridge and left it unattended during time of abduction.
10. On each of the Fridays on which murders were committed, she had driven the car near Coolidge and left it unattended.
11. On day following abduction she bought car of her own, a grey Renault.
12. She was assisted in purchase by a man called 'Pete.'
13. Pete drove off in the Renault with her.
14. They were gone for four hours.
15. Pete identified as Peter Mellish of 113 Cluny Avenue.
16. During routine check, Mellish lied about his movements on afternoon of 5th June.
17. Mellish is self-employed, good craftsman, versatile. Unmarried, travels, has lived with mother for last nine months. Attractive to women. Drives other cars at times. In snooker final at Army and Navy club— possible sadism: incident of cruelty to cat at club when member prevented him from stamping on it.
18. Description reasonable likeness to photo picture. Age group and build fit.

Jordan recovered from a bout of coughing and cleared his throat. "We've got a strong suspect and a suspect car. How do we connect the two?"

"Mrs. Stringer's the common denominator," said Anders. "If he's got anything to do with it, either he pinches the car and takes it back where he finds it, or she lets him have it. All we can say for sure at the moment is that she knows him and went for a ride with him in *her* car, not the Austin."

"Maybe it's time we put it to her. If she says she lent it to him, we'd be getting somewhere."

"Supposing she's mixed up in it? I know it's unlikely but it's happened before. We've kept right away from her and we don't know much about her. We know they haven't met since we put a tail on him, although he's made one or two calls from public boxes, so he may have contacted her. We can pull him in now and have a go at him and we could put a bit of pressure on her."

"It might work."

"On the other hand, if he's as fly as I think he is, *he* won't break. We might get something from the lab, but I wouldn't like to bank on it. Personally I think we want a bit more and I'd give it a day or two. What d'you say?"

"It's tantalizing," said Jordan, "but I suppose you're right. Even if he is identified, I doubt whether it would stick without the car. What about the clothing chummy was wearing at the time? Mellish says he went to the tobacconist's near where he lives. There's just a chance someone there will remember seeing him."

"I didn't do anything about it before in case it got back to him. I'll get Carver and Hudson to go down there."

The newsagents, tobacconists and confectioners in Cluny Avenue was owned by a Mr. Charles Gillings, a thin, pedantic little man, who ran the establishment with a rather austere efficiency. His wife and his widowed sister-in-law helped in the shop. He also employed a nineteen-year-old girl assistant.

Just after five o'clock in the afternoon he was hovering in the background trying to sort out those who wanted to make a quick purchase from the lingerers and undecideds, when two large men appeared in the doorway. As the shop began to clear, the one with a slightly bent nose and furrowed forehead moved to the corner close to the counter. He spoke quietly. "Mr. Gillings?"

"Yes."

The man produced a police warrant card. "Detective Chief Inspector Carver and Detective-Sergeant Hudson. I'd like a few words with you in private."

Mr. Gillings wasn't very favourably disposed towards the police. Twice in the last three months he had been caught in a radar trap. "You want to speak to me? What about?"

"Not here, sir."

Gillings shrugged. "I can't think what it can be. I'm rather busy. Can you make it later, say nearer seven?"

"I'm afraid not. This is very urgent."

"If it's about this missing girl, the police have already been round."

"I'm well aware of that and it is about her. Shall we not waste time?"

Gillings shrugged again and led them to a room at the back of the shop.

"Can you tell me who was serving in the shop on the afternoon of Tuesday, 5th June?"

"If it was between half past one and half past three, it would have been Tina, my assistant. It's quiet then and the rest of us take a break."

"There'd be nobody else serving?"

"I doubt it."

"Where's Tina now?"

"At home probably. She lives just round the corner in Pentland Avenue, number 33."

Carver reached into his pocket and brought out a photograph. "Do you know this man?"

Gillings squinted at it. "He looks like somebody who comes into the shop occasionally but I can't say I know him."

"Have you ever seen him in a blue shirt and slacks?"

"May have, but I never remember what people wear."

"What is Tina's surname?"

"Stuart. Tina Stuart."

"We'll pay her a visit. Thank you, Mr. Gillings, and please treat this matter in confidence."

"Sure, I will," said Gillings, who by now had begun to realize that this was more than a routine enquiry and that somebody on his own doorstep could be involved.

A little over a hundred yards away, Mellish was searching in his mother's wardrobe. He continued to rummage round until he found what he was looking for: a hideous blond wig which she had worn on occasions some years ago until even she had realized that it made her look ridiculous.

It didn't do anything for him either, but it certainly changed his appearance and, as long as he kept out of the light as much as possible, it would look reasonably natural. If by chance somebody noticed him coming away or boarding a train, he would see a long-haired blond character in a mac. Most people only noticed the obvious and sometimes not even that.

A short, stocky man with ginger hair and bristling eyebrows answered the door at 33 Pentland Avenue.

"Does Miss Tina Stuart live here?" asked Carver.

"Yes."

"You're Mr. Stuart, her father?"

"Yes. What is it?"

Carver flashed his warrant card and introduced himself and Hudson.

"What do you want her for?"

"It's nothing she's done. She may be able to help us in our enquiries—identify somebody for us."

"Oh! I suppose you'd better come in. She's having tea."

They waited in the hall and after a few moments she came out to them, a well-built girl with good features but, thought Carver, utterly devoid of sex appeal. She looked at the photograph while her father hovered in the background, and then said without any show of interest: "Seen him now and again. I don't think he lives far from the shop."

"What about between one and three-thirty last Tuesday week?

I know it's asking much but can you recollect if he called then?"

"I can't remember all that far back. He might have."

"Would you remember what he was wearing at any time?"

"No, I don't think so."

"Have you ever seen him in a blue shirt and slacks?"

"I don't remember anything he wore."

Carver turned toward the door. "Pity. Oh, well, thanks anyway."

"I'll tell you who might remember."

They moved back again.

"Marge Wilkins. She often comes in the shop in the afternoons—talking and that."

"She's a friend of yours?"

"Sort of."

"Why should she remember?"

"She notices anything with two legs and trousers, especially if it's not bad-looking."

"Where can we find Marge?"

"If she's at home—Tunbridge Avenue. I don't know the number but it's the last house on the left going towards the playground for kids."

Hudson made a note and Carver said: "Thank you, Miss Stuart. You've been a great help."

At quarter past six Mrs. Mellish came home somewhat dispirited about a losing session that had taken most of her spare cash. Mellish, glancing at the time to see how long he'd got, thought he'd watch television for another twenty minutes.

"Hallo, Pete," she said. "Shall I get you something?"

"I've had it. I'm going out."

"Anywhere special?"

"Somewhere that wouldn't interest you."

"And you don't want anything?"

"I've already told you—no."

"Oh, all right."

She hovered behind him until eventually he turned in his seat. "For Christ sake, what's the matter with you?"

"I was going to the Bull tonight."

"Well, go on then."

She sniffed several times and started to wander from the room.

"Oh," he said, "I suppose you've blued it all again. You and your bloody bingo! You want to learn to gamble on yourself and not a bloody card."

He felt in his pocket, folded up three pound notes and threw them at her.

"Thanks, Pete. You're a good boy."

His lips twisted sardonically as he turned his attention to the box again.

Carver and Hudson were lucky. Marge Wilkins was at home but only just. She had her coat on and in another two minutes they would have missed her. Unlike Tina Stuart she was not particularly well built but she had an inviting look in her eyes and a generous mouth.

"I understand that you're observant," said Carver, "and clever at noticing things."

"Where d'you hear that?"

"Never mind. You could be of great help to us. I believe you often call at the newsagents in Cluny Avenue for a chat with your friend there, Miss Stuart?"

"That's right."

Carver produced the photograph. "Can you remember ever seeing this man?"

She took the photograph from him. "Oh yes. I've seen him. He's rather dishy."

"When was the last time you saw him?"

"It must have been over a week ago." Disappointment crept into her voice. "Has he been up to something then?"

"We're not sure yet. Did you see him in the shop?"

"Yes, that's right. There was only Tina and me there."

"About what time would that have been?"

"Two or just before, I'd say."

"Now, think carefully. What was he wearing?"

"I don't have to think. He had on an open-neck shirt with short sleeves and a nice, tight-fitting pair of slacks."

"What colour?"

"Blue."

"You can be sure of that after all this time?"

She shrugged. "As I said, he's dishy, and I've seen him before. This blue outfit looked real smart. He winked at me as he went out!"

"Thank you. Thank you very much. You won't mind if we come and see you again?"

"Any time!"

"What a bit of luck," said Hudson as they drove away. "All we want now is the last piece in the jig-saw—the car!"

Carver lifted the microphone. "MHQ from One-niner, over."

"Go ahead, One-niner."

"For Mr. Anders. Blue is a winner."

There was a pause and then Anders's voice came over. "Fred! We'll move in now. Go to the house and detain. I'm on my way down."

"Roger," said Carver and replaced the microphone.

At half past six Mellish switched off the television, stood up and stretched his limbs. Then he went up to his room and collected his parcel. There was still the suction pump to get but he knew where he could borrow one on the way.

He rarely bothered to say anything before he went out and he already had his hand on the door catch when he heard a resounding crash from the kitchen. He hesitated for a moment and then, leaving his parcel in the hall, went to investigate.

His mother was lying in a twisted heap on the floor with a mass of broken crockery round her. "What've you bloody well done now?" he asked.

There was no reply and when he bent over her and straightened her out, she stared at him and made curious globby sounds. One side of her face hung loose. He knew what had happened and cursed.

But it wouldn't stop him. Why should it? Doctors couldn't help. It was all arranged and maybe he wouldn't get another chance. In any case, he was looking forward to it.

He dragged her into the living-room and, lifting her on to the settee, put a cushion under her head. Her one good eye followed him pleadingly.

"You'll be all right there, Ma," he said. "Won't be long. I'll get a doctor."

Leaving the house, he walked down the road and the officer who was intent on watching the car didn't see him go.

A few minutes later Carver and Hudson arrived and when there was no answer at the front of the house Hudson went round to the back. Shortly after, he opened the front door. "He's not here," he said, "but we'll need a doctor. The old lady's had a stroke."

Anders, in the front passenger seat of the CID car, had forgotten he was tired. Half a mile from their destination he called out suddenly: "Hold it!" and the detective who was driving braked and said: "What's up, sir?"

Anders was looking back. "That was him we just passed—Peter Mellish, carrying a parcel."

The driver turned the car round and for a few moments they followed, making sure. Then they closed and got out. Mellish looked up in surprise.

"Peter Mellish?" said Anders.

"Yes? What's it to you?"

"Detective-Superintendent Anders. I want you to come with me to the police station. I think you can help me with certain enquiries."

"Enquiries? What bloody enquiries? I'm on my way some-where."

They moved closer. "That's right—to the police station."

He tensed and his eyes moved from one to the other. "If you say so," he said, "but it's a bloody liberty."

CHAPTER 9

After the first sudden shock, Mellish sat in the back of the car and slowly regained control of himself. He couldn't imagine how they had got to him, but they had. Mavis? Had she said anything, told them he had driven her car on his own? Unlikely, very unlikely! There'd be no reason and she wouldn't. Anyway, why should they connect her with him? It must be the old girl and the kid. They'd knocked him on description, and without the car that wouldn't hold up.

He wasn't the type who softened under pressure and made it easy for them. In a way it could be interesting: a battle of wits, a challenge he could take up and win.

They put him in a room with plain green walls, a high, barred window, a table and three bentwood chairs, and left him for about fifteen minutes with a uniformed constable who stood by the door and said nothing.

He still had his parcel and they hadn't taken anything else from him. He lit a cigarette and extended the packet to the constable, who shook his head but moved a small metal ashtray from the window sill to the table.

Mellish was stubbing out the remains of the cigarette when

Anders and Carver came in, followed by a thick-set sergeant with a prominent bald patch on his head. The constable withdrew.

"First things first," said Anders. "Turn out your pockets, Mr. Mellish."

"You're joking!"

"You think so?"

"Am I under arrest for something or not?"

"You're a suspect helping us with our enquiries."

"Then I don't have to stop here? I'm free to go?"

"Theoretically yes, in practice no. Now turn out your pockets before we have to do it for you."

Reluctantly Mellish stood up and, with insolent deliberation, put the contents of his pockets in a neat pile on the table. Then he stared fixedly at Carver who ran his hands over him to make sure he'd left nothing.

There were five pounds, fifty-three pence in cash, a gas cigarette lighter, a penknife, a driving licence and sundry papers.

"What's in the parcel?" asked Anders.

"A raincoat and a wig."

Carver opened it, held up the wig and handed it to Anders.

"What did you want that for?"

"That's my business. There's no law against carrying a wig and a raincoat, is there?"

"Could be, in certain circumstances."

Mellish sat down. "I'd like my cigarettes and lighter!"

"I expect you would," said Anders and turned to the sergeant. "List it all and bag it."

There was complete silence while this was being done and, when he had finished, the sergeant pushed the form and a ballpoint pen across the table to Mellish. "Sign that if it's correct, please."

"I'm signing nothing."

Anders pulled the form towards him and signed it, and when Carver had added his signature the sergeant collected the property and left them.

Anders sat at the table opposite Mellish and Carver occupied a chair to the side.

"Now, Mr. Mellish," said Anders, "on the afternoon of Tuesday, 5th June, a girl of seven was abducted and taken to Sethley Common. The man responsible was interrupted before he could do any real harm to the child. You answer the description of that man."

"Me and a thousand others. So that's it, is it? I'll answer all your questions in one go. It wasn't me."

"Where were you at the time?"

"I don't know what you mean by 'the time,' but somebody's already asked me, put it on a form. I was at home."

"Doing what?"

"Changing the cylinder head gasket on my car. You don't do that in five minutes."

"You're sure of that?"

"Of course I'm sure."

"The engine of your car has been examined by experienced mechanics and they are quite certain that the cylinder head hasn't been removed for months."

"Oh yes?" said Mellish, apparently unmoved. "When was this?"

"Early yesterday morning."

"It's up to them to think what they like. I know I did."

"They didn't *think*. Anyway, to go on. Your mother left the house at one-thirty and didn't return until nearly six, so she can't vouch for you. Is there anybody else who can?"

"I don't know. I haven't asked anybody. I didn't think I would have to."

"Surely somebody round there would have seen you working on your car?"

"Not necessarily. Most of them go round with their eyes shut."

"There is somebody who doesn't. What did you do with the blue shirt and blue slacks you were wearing?"

"I've never worn a blue shirt and slacks. What are you trying on now?"

"You went to the tobacconist's some time between one-thirty and two. We have a witness who says you were wearing them then."

Mellish cursed himself. It had been a mistake to mention calling for cigarettes but it had seemed a good idea at the time. "I've never worn a blue shirt and slacks. They must have mistaken me for somebody else."

"A bit of coincidence, isn't it?" said Carver. "You admit going to the shop at that time and then your double goes in just before or after?"

"I don't know. I'm not interested."

"You ought to be," said Anders. "When did you last see Mrs. Stringer?"

Mellish sensed the trap. He was talking too much. But this needed some answer. As if amused at some secret thought, he gave a short laugh. "A few days ago. I helped her buy a car from Sullivan's."

"Why?"

"Because she asked me to."

"When did she ask you?"

"What's all this got to do with it?"

"Quite a lot and you won't do yourself any good by hedging."

"If it's of any interest, I did a tiling job on her bathroom months ago—getting on for a year—and the other day I bumped into her in the High Street. She said she'd been thinking of getting in touch with me about another job and she mentioned as well that she wanted to buy a small car for herself. I asked her what sort and she said she didn't know anything about cars, so I offered to help."

"Then you went for a ride with her for four hours?"

"What of it? She wanted to get the hang of the car and she gave me three quid."

"And you made fifty on the side with Mr. Myall."

"Did he tell you that, the old bastard?"

"He did."

"If you believe what he says, you'll believe anything."

92

"Why did you get a car from him if you think he's so unreliable?"

"I can judge a car for myself. I don't have to take his word for it."

Anders studied him for a few moments. "How many other times have you seen Mrs. Stringer?"

"I haven't."

"So if she says differently, she's also lying?"

"She couldn't have done," said Mellish, again hiding the uneasy thought. "Why should she?"

"Where were you going when we stopped you?"

"That's my business."

"You've some reason for not wanting us to know?"

Mellish had been doing some rapid thinking. If they hadn't already seen Mavis, they almost certainly would. But as long as she didn't say anything about his driving her car, so what! He could say he lied to protect her good name, so that her husband wouldn't know. He'd said enough now anyway. If only he could get word to her!

"I thought you were supposed to caution me?" he asked.

"We haven't arrested you yet, have we?"

With an almost imperceptible nod from Anders, Carver pulled his chair forward. "Let's go over it again," he said. "Now..."

"I'm not going over anything. You've had your answers. I want to get out of here."

For an hour they continued to question him but they got no further. So they left him and the constable came back.

"I think I may have made a mistake," said Anders. "Perhaps we should have seen Mrs. Stringer first."

Carver, who had favoured this approach earlier, felt a duty to be magnanimous. "I don't know. As you said, she might have warned him off and he could have skipped. We can still see her before any damage is done. But what about his mother? We haven't told him yet."

"He knows. He must have dragged her in from the kitchen

93

and left her on the settee. What a bastard! We'll spring it on him later. You're sure you didn't miss anything at his place?"

"There certainly weren't any blue slacks or shirts, or anything else that would tie up."

They went to the Stringers' home but there was no one there, and an hour later the house was still in darkness. "We'll keep calling," said Anders.

When they went back to the interview room, Mellish made a show of indignation. "I've had enough of this. I want a solicitor. And I'm going to see my MP."

Anders ignored him and sat down. "How was your mother when you left her?"

"She wasn't feeling too good, but she said she'd be all right. Why?"

"You dragged her in from the kitchen where she had fallen and left her on the settee."

"What are you talking about?"

"You didn't even bother to clear up all the broken china."

"Here," said Mellish, getting to his feet. "Broken china? What's happened to her?"

"She's had a stroke and is now in hospital."

"Now, you look here!" Mellish warmed to the act. "I'm going out and I'm going to see her. Why didn't you tell me before?"

"Don't push your luck, Mellish," said Carver quietly.

But Anders had seen ahead. He visualized the headlines: "Callous police behaviour stops man from seeing dying mother." He said firmly: "Sit down. You'll be allowed to see her."

Mellish subsided slowly on to his chair and Anders looked up at Carver. "Ask the Station Sergeant to come in with the necessary."

Carver left the room and Anders waited for him to return with the sergeant before he said to Mellish: "I am now arresting you on suspicion of being the person who, on Tuesday, 5th June of this year, in the borough of Forebridge, abducted Peggy Finney, a child under fourteen years. You need not say anything unless you wish to but anything you do say will be taken down and may be given in evidence."

"You're wasting your time," said Mellish. "You've got the wrong bloke," and the sergeant made the necessary entry in the apprehension book.

When the apprehension form had been completed, Anders said: "You will now be allowed to see your mother, under escort."

Anders was faced with a difficult decision. What extent of freedom should Mellish be allowed when visiting his mother? It would hardly improve Mrs. Mellish's condition to see her son in handcuffs. Also there still wasn't enough evidence to charge him and any man who was paraded in manacles through a hospital and who was later set free, uncharged, would have a reasonable case for damages. On the other hand, Mellish was a strong suspect. If he was guilty, he might be desperate and seize on the first chance of escape. To have their man in the bag and then lose him so soon was unthinkable. Jordan would go spare!

In the end, having established the fact that the ward to be visited had only one entrance and that it was on the fourth floor, he decided to compromise. Mellish would be handcuffed but all the time he was open to public view the handcuffs would be covered by the raincoat he had brought with the wig. At the ward door, the handcuffs would be removed and then put on again when Mellish returned after having seen his mother.

As an added precaution, four police officers were to be stationed in the grounds in case Mellish attempted to escape from one of the windows.

But while there was still a good chance of acquittal, Mellish had no intention of attempting to escape. It would want some explaining if he were subsequently caught, and he wasn't going to lead a life on the run unless it was absolutely necessary.

He submitted willingly to the arrangements, all the time concentrating his mind on devising some way of getting word to Mavis Stringer undetected. He guessed they hadn't seen her or, if they had, they'd got nothing out of her. If she had said anything incriminating they wouldn't have been slow in coming out with it.

Two plain-clothes officers accompanied him to the ward doors. One looked as if he could cover the ground pretty quickly and the other was built like an all-in wrestler. They took off the handcuffs and Mellish left them.

The approach to the ward had various rooms on either side and in one, with the door open, sat a nurse at a desk. Mellish assumed an expression of almost pious sincerity as she looked up at him. "I've just heard about my mother, Mrs. Mellish."

She rose from her chair, a pretty Malayan who immediately gave the impression of being politely correct and yet at the same time anxious to please.

"Mrs. Mellish? I will show you. But you must be very quiet. The other patients are trying to sleep."

"I understand." He smiled at her. "I'll be as quiet as I can."

He glanced back at the outer door as he followed her but the detectives hadn't come inside. Whatever he did would have to be quick, and he already had an idea.

She was propped up in bed, one eye half closed and the other slightly moving in its socket. One side of her mouth sagged.

"Hallo, Ma," he whispered.

Her lips barely opened but she said something which he thought ended in "Pete."

"You'll be all right in here, Ma. Best place for you until you get better."

Her moving eye became fixed in a vacant stare and she mumbled incoherently. But he wasn't thinking of her now. On the table beside the next bed was a pad of notepaper, half hidden by a "get well" card, and on the shelf underneath, a few envelopes. Calmly he strolled round and took a sheet from the pad and an envelope, and he was lucky again when he found a pencil. He was about to return to the chair by his mother's bed when he was conscious of a woman in another bed watching him, and he went over to her. "Will you tell this lady that I have borrowed a sheet of paper and an envelope from her? I've got to write an urgent message for my mother." The woman nodded and tried to smile.

After a quick look towards the doors, he sat by his mother again and wrote feverishly. He addressed the envelope, sealed it and then he loosened his belt. Fortunately they hadn't taken it from him yet. Along the lining on each side of the fastening was a slim pocket in which he kept a number of currency notes for emergency, the habit of the experienced traveller. There was nothing like ready cash for making you self-reliant. He took out two pounds, fastened the belt again and waited.

It wasn't long before the nurse appeared. "I think you ought to be going now."

He stood up. "Yes, of course. Nurse, I wonder if you could do me a favour." He pointed to the letter and the two pound notes he had left on the bedside table. "I know it's asking a lot, but can you get somebody to deliver that for me by hand? It's a message from my mother to someone who is leaving in the morning and I can't possibly get there myself in time. I've left a couple of pounds for somebody's trouble."

He watched her as she went to the table and looked at the address.

"I'd be most grateful."

"Well..."

"It's not breaking any rules, is it? I wouldn't want you to do that."

"I will try and have it sent for you."

"Thank you, Nurse. Thank you very much. And thank you too for all you're doing for my mother."

He walked towards the entrance, reflecting on his luck. But it wasn't all luck, some of it was his doing. He was also conscious of the risks. He had to trust the nurse. Somebody else might open the letter. Later, if he were charged, she might remember the incident and tell the police. But they were all risks he would have to take.

He needn't have worried. The nurse delivered the letter herself just after eight o'clock in the morning and within the week had left the hospital to return to her own country.

CHAPTER 10

Mavis Stringer waited for over an hour and her anxiety grew with each passing second until doubt gave way to certainty. He wasn't coming!

Panic seized her when she visualized a world without him and she started the engine and had driven off before she realized what she was doing. A squeal of brakes, followed by an angry shout, brought her partly to her senses, and further up the road she stopped.

The indecision was torture. She knew where he lived. She couldn't go in but she could drive by. Something might come of it. But when she got there, his car was outside. Perhaps it had broken down? Even so, over an hour? He would have had plenty of time.

Nothing mattered any more now. What could she do? George was at Blackpool at a conference, not that he could have helped. But she didn't want to be by herself. Then she thought of Helen Reeves. She lived alone and they'd always got on well enough.

She stayed the night with Helen Reeves and returned home just after ten the following morning. There were three letters on the mat. One of them, unstamped, and addressed in pencil, was for her.

"*My darling,*" he had written. "*This is to tell you how sorry I am about tonight. The fact is the police have arrested me and are trying to make me admit that I'm the man who kidnapped that girl. Me, I ask you! Apparently I answer the description and they're trying to pin it on me. They've got to find somebody. The trouble is that a car something like your Austin was involved and if they find out I've been in it they'll charge me. What's more the real culprit will get away. I'd get off because it's so stupid but we could say goodbye to the job in Newcastle. So don't try and contact me for a bit and don't let them know I've ever been in your husband's car. They know I helped you buy your Renault. I told them I'd run into you in the High Street the other day and that we talked about me doing another tiling job for you and you told me you wanted to buy a car and knew nothing about them. I said I'd done a job for you previously and hadn't seen you since. It's awful darling being like this but I know what they are. I'm writing this in hospital. They've let me come here because my mother's had a stroke. I am going to try and get a nurse to deliver it as they mustn't know.*

"*How I missed you this evening darling. As soon as it's safe I'll get in touch.*

All my love, Peter.
P.S. Get rid of this letter darling in case they find it."

She read it through again, horrified and yet relieved.

Then a knock came on the door. For a few moments she found it difficult to breathe. She screwed up the letter and held it to her as if whoever was outside could see right through the door. Then she hurried to the sitting-room looking round for her handbag until she remembered she had left it in the hall.

Get rid of it, he had said, but she couldn't—his first letter to her! She went back to the hall, and as she snatched her handbag from the side table she could see that they had come into the storm porch—two large shadows against the frosted glass. She retreated into the sitting-room and was looking for a suitable place in her handbag when, in her ignorance, a thought struck her. Suppose they were to search her? Her handbag would be the first place they would go to.

There was another knock and the door bell rang. Hurriedly she went to the kitchen and poked the letter behind an electric spit which stood on the working surface near the window. Then she leaned against the wall, taking several deep breaths. She had to control herself. She had to for his sake, for their sakes.

Again there was a knock and with reasonable composure she went to the door and opened it. They were police all right: both large men in quiet lounge suits. They didn't look unfriendly, but she hated them.

"Mrs. Mavis Stringer?"

"Yes?"

"We're police officers, Mrs. Stringer. I'm Detective-Superintendent Anders and this is Detective-Sergeant Hudson." He showed her his warrant card. "May we come in?"

She stood aside. "What is it? Has something happened to my husband?"

"No. As far as we know your husband is perfectly all right. He's at business, is he?"

"He's in Blackpool at a conference."

"How long will he be gone?"

"He's coming back the day after tomorrow."

"And he went?"

"Yesterday morning. Do you want to see him?"

"We may do."

They had moved to the sitting-room and she noticed that the sergeant had his pocket-book out. "What was it you wanted then?"

"I believe you know a man named Peter Mellish?"

She marshalled her thoughts, reflecting that it was not only what she said but how she said it. She mustn't let her emotions give her away.

"I know a man named Mellish. He tiled my bathroom some time ago and the other day I met him in the High Street and he agreed to help me buy a car."

"How many times had you seen him in between?"

"I hadn't. What makes you ask?"

"After he went with you to buy the car, you went for a ride in it together?"

"Yes, so that I could get used to the controls."

"It took you four hours?"

She felt a flush spreading from her neck and wondered if it showed. "I can't remember the time but I know we went a long way."

"Where did you go?"

"Round the country somewhere. It was a lovely day." The panic was starting again. If only she knew what they knew! Had somebody seen them at the weekend bungalow?

"Going back to your car, why did you buy it when you had full use of your husband's Austin, a much better car?"

"I wanted one of my own." Annoyance gave her confidence. "I'm beginning to find your questions most objectionable. What has it to do with you whether I buy a car for myself or not?"

Anders nodded sympathetically. "I'm sorry if we seem unnecessarily inquisitive. The truth is, we have reason to believe that Peter Mellish is the man responsible among other things for abducting a small child on the 5th June."

Just in time she prevented herself making a vigorous protest, but the sudden flash which came into her eyes didn't go unnoticed by Anders. "Are you sure?" she said. "He didn't seem that sort of man. I can't really believe it's possible."

"Perhaps you don't want to believe it?"

"I don't know what you mean by that, but I suppose I don't. I rather liked him."

"Has he ever been in your husband's car?"

How much longer could she stand this? "No, he hasn't."

"Perhaps he has taken it without your knowledge."

"No. How could he? Do you mind going now?"

102

Anders walked to the window and looked out at the garden. "I don't believe you have any children, Mrs. Stringer?"

"Is that supposed to be a crime?"

"The child who was abducted would undoubtedly have been murdered if the man concerned hadn't been interrupted. Another girl age nine years—I believe your husband knows the parents—has been missing since the 4th June. There is little doubt that she has been murdered by the same man. Over the last six months, and on days when your car was near Coolidge, three girls were murdered in Coolidge, almost certainly by the same man. If Mellish is innocent, he has nothing to fear. But if he is not and if you, in some mistaken feeling of loyalty, are withholding information about him, you will have a lot on your conscience."

Her head swam and she was glad he wasn't looking at her and that she had her back to the sergeant. Then in a rush of anger she said: "How dare you? You're suggesting that I'm not telling the truth! How dare you?"

Anders turned slowly and reached into his pocket for a pad of paper and his pen. He wrote on the top sheet, tore it off and put it on the table. "If you do remember anything that will help us, you can contact me at that number. You say Mr. Stringer will be home the day after tomorrow?"

"Yes, but it's no good seeing him. He's never even seen . . . Mr. Mellish."

"I'd gathered that much. Good morning, Mrs. Stringer."

They sat outside in the car and Anders let out a deep sigh. "I backed a loser. It was too pat. 'I met him in the High Street.' Somehow he got to her and I'd like to know how, unless he anticipated it. Not that it matters much now."

"I can't see how he could have contacted her," said Hudson. "The only time he was out of their sight was when he went into the ward at the hospital."

"And she didn't come home all night. It's a mystery. Anyway, we've got plenty to do without worrying about that now. Let's get back and fix up this identity parade."

From behind the curtains Mavis Stringer watched them go, and when she moved away a spell of dizziness forced her to sit down. The things they'd said! They couldn't be true! They couldn't!

She got up and ran out to the kitchen. Retrieving the letter, she read it again. "... and the real culprit will get away. How I missed you this evening ... My darling"

Then the glorious feeling of relief! The Murray child, she knew about that. She knew the day. She had good cause to. All the afternoon they had been together right up to the time when they'd been seen in the quarry, so it couldn't be Peter. She felt ashamed of her small spasm of doubt.

But she couldn't tell them either. They wouldn't believe her. They'd say she was trying to cover up and she'd have to admit she'd been lying, that he had been in the car. But it wasn't him, that was what mattered. And as long as she said nothing, perhaps they could do nothing.

Again she read the letter through and then put it back in the envelope and tried to think where she could hide it, somewhere nobody would think of looking. For at least ten minutes she walked about with it in her hand, rejecting one place after another. And then, remembering the postscript, she realized how stupid she was being. He was right. It wasn't worth the risk.

She went to the kitchen and found a box of matches but before she watched it burning she read it through once more.

They had put him in a cell with a high, grilled window and a wooden bench running the length of the wall, and had given him a Dunlopillo mattress to put on the bench, some bedclothes and a pair of striped pyjamas.

He was awake in the morning when, with a clanking of keys, his cell door opened and an enormous, red-faced constable entered and dropped a brown suit, a pair of brown shoes and a clean shirt on the end of the bunk. Mellish, sitting up, recognized them as his own.

"Where's the stuff they took away yesterday?" he asked.

The constable surveyed him with apparent distaste. "You'd better ask 'em. I've left your electric razor out by the wash bowl. Get cracking."

The same constable brought him some breakfast: two sausages, an egg and some baked beans, and several times the peephole in the door was uncovered and someone looked through.

He had made up his mind to say as little as possible. So far it hadn't been difficult; no one had wanted to speak to him. Now and again he wondered what they were cooking up but the success he'd had in smuggling out the letter had given him added confidence. With all of them against him, watching him, making so bloody sure about everything, he'd fooled them. They just didn't know what they were up against. And when he got out, he'd clear off, change his name. Whatever happened, they'd never hold him. He'd need a solicitor though—if they pressed it. Lewis Wynn was the one. He knew about him. He had a reputation for getting you off the hook.

The bloody woman in Sethley Park, that's what they were banking on. But he thought he had the answer. He'd never been inside before but he'd made a point of looking things up and finding out what they could and what they couldn't do.

About an hour after he'd had breakfast Anders, Jordan and Carver came in. From a buff file he was holding, Anders extracted a photograph of Angela Murray and put it in front of Mellish. "Have you seen this girl anywhere?"

Mellish looked at it and shook his head. "Never seen her before. But aren't you supposed to caution me first? Not that it matters, I suppose."

"Take it as read," said Anders and made a note of the time and remarks made. "Can you account for your movements on the afternoon of the 5th June?"

"You're joking! I was probably doing a job for somebody."

"You can't provide some proof of what you were doing?"

"No, and I don't intend to try."

Anders made more notes and then indicated Jordan. "This is Detective Chief Superintendent Jordan and he's going to ask you a few questions."

Jordan made an entry in his own book and then, referring to it, said: "Where were you on the afternoon of the 9th January?"

"How can I remember that?"

"Were you in the Coolidge district?"

"I shouldn't think so."

"Why?"

"Because I don't go there often."

"Why?"

"Lay off! I'm not saying any more until I've seen my solicitor."

There was a moment's silence and then Anders said: "All in good time. Meanwhile, if you've got nothing to hide, answer the questions."

"What about the afternoon of the 23rd February?" said Jordan.

"No comment."

"And the 6th April?"

"No comment."

"Haven't you got a diary?"

"No."

"How do you remember the jobs you've got in hand then?"

"That's my business."

"You work freelance for other people?"

"You know I do."

"And you keep reasonably busy?"

"Do I?"

"Mr. Mellish," said Jordan, "it is understandable that you may not remember your precise movements on the dates mentioned, but your attitude in refusing to make any attempt suggests that you well know where you were and an admission would be incriminating?"

"Suggest what you like."

Jordan made a further note, then shut his book and glanced at Anders.

Anders placed a small red book on the table. "Would you care to refer to that?"

Mellish experienced a momentary anger and then he realized that this was what they wanted. "Where did you get it?"

"In the front pocket of your dustcoat. If you refer to it, you will see that there are entries but none for the others mentioned."

"That means nothing. I don't put in everything."

"Some time this morning I shall ask you to take part in an identity parade, but before then we'll give you the chance to contact a solicitor to advise you."

"I don't need his advice about that. I can tell you now. I'm not going on one."

They stared at him. "Are you serious?"

"Of course I am. You'll fix it so that they know me before they start. And why should I? Why should I have to prove I'm innocent?"

"You realize that a refusal will go against you?"

"Not as much as if someone picks me out—even when they *are* put up to it."

They could see he meant it.

"Perhaps your solicitor will have different views," said Anders, and they left him.

Lewis Wynn demurred at first and then, sensing something big, agreed to see Mellish. He arrived just after ten, and when in fact Anders was interviewing Mrs. Stringer.

He was a man of forty, tall and, with the aid of an expensive tailor, managed to look reasonably slim. He had a prominent nose, sharp eyes and a loose mouth. To him there was no such thing as dirty money and the only moral principles which concerned him were those which couldn't be covered up. He excused himself with the claim that he used every lawful means at his disposal in the interests of his clients, but he neglected to mention that in many cases it was almost impossible to prove whether the means were lawful or not. He owned a large house with a swimming pool, a bungalow by the sea and ran a Mercedes and a Rover.

He listened to Mellish and would have wagered heavily that most of the time he was lying. As he saw it so far, the case was critically balanced but he didn't underestimate the police. He was also rather concerned at Mellish's refusal to appear on an identification parade. Mellish was adamant.

"This Mrs. Stringer," said Wynn and paused. "This Mrs. Stringer! It's true, is it, that you didn't see her between the tiling job you did for her and when she asked you to help buy a car for her?"

"Everything I tell you is true."

"Hmm!" For a fleeting moment a chilling doubt ran through the solicitor. There was something uncomfortably odd about this one. "You say they asked you where you were on a number of different dates. Is it true you can't account for any of them?"

"I haven't bothered to think about it."

"Well, you must if you want me to represent you. You'll have to make some effort."

"Why? There are plenty of blokes about like me and all I drive is a red Mini."

"Frankly I don't think they've got enough to charge you yet but they won't have finished. If there *is* anything more, I want to know about it first."

"How can there be anything more? All they've really got on me is that I look like this picture and they'll try and get someone to pick me out."

"I can hardly believe that, but we'll find out in due course."

Wynn got up and surveyed Mellish with the interest of a connoisseur. He couldn't quite make up his mind whether or not he was doing the right thing. Feelings ran high not only in the district but the country. Then he decided. "Say nothing now," he said. "Nothing more at all. Don't try and be clever. If you *are* charged, we will plead not guilty and reserve our defence."

* * *

"He's our man," said Jordan. "I've never been more sure of anything. D'you mean to say all you found at his place was that notebook?"

Anders looked at Carver who, with two others, had searched Mellish's home and Carver shook his head. "Nothing of any significance. His clothes have been to the lab and so far they haven't come up with anything."

"What about the girl who says she saw him in his blue gear?"

"He was sharp there," said Anders. "He said that if the real culprit was so much like him, it was quite possible for the girl to be mistaken. We need a positive identification but he's made that difficult."

"Difficult but not impossible," said Jordan. "His refusal has opened another door to us, not so decisive but one the court will probably accept in the circumstances. Get your witnesses here and take him out in the yard."

"It sounds easy enough but I don't trust this quiet manner of his. He might smell a rat and if he gets violent or covers his face we'd have to use force and that wouldn't look so good, would it?"

"Make sure he doesn't smell a rat," said Jordan.

In his cell Mellish was feeling quietly confident. It had jarred a bit when they had produced his notebook but there was nothing incriminating there, and the fact that they hadn't mentioned Mavis again was a good sign. They hadn't got anywhere with her. They were floundering, clutching at straws, and he was beginning to doubt whether they would charge him. He had considered the possibility, and the thought of being kept in custody for a short period didn't disturb him. Now he'd got a solicitor, they would have to treat him all right and provide him with books and papers to pass the time.

Suddenly it occurred to him that he ought to have asked about his mother; it would have looked good. But he hadn't thought of her and he hadn't even mentioned her to Wynn.

There was a button on the door and he pressed it. After a few moments the door opened and a constable looked in.

"I want to see somebody about my mother who's in hospital," said Mellish.

The constable nodded, looked at him with undisguised interest and then shut and locked the door again. Another fifteen minutes and Carver came in with a large detective Mellish hadn't seen before.

"I understand you're asking about your mother?" said Carver.

"That's right. I want to see her."

"This way then," said Carver and, with the large officer bringing up the rear, Mellish followed him out of the cell.

They led him through a bare spacious room with a tiled floor, and a uniformed constable unlocked a grille door for them to pass through into a narrow passage. At the end of the passage was an open door, and daylight.

Carver, who reached the doorway first, hesitated, blocking the way, and Mellish didn't notice his slight nod. Then Carver stepped aside and Mellish saw the woman from Sethley Common standing there with Anders a few feet away.

"Have you seen this man before?" asked Anders and, as the woman stared intently and nodded, Mellish erupted. With clenched fists he swung round and back again. "You bastards! You . . ." He made a move forward and then Carver hit him, his fist sinking deep into the solar plexus. Carver's strength more than matched his size and Mellish sank to his knees with a hollow groan.

"I'm sorry you had to see that," said Anders to Mrs. Conway.

"I'm not," she said. "I'm glad."

Limping with pain, Mellish was taken back to his cell and left there. The paralysing effect of the blow would pass but a new hatred of the police and of Carver in particular would stay with him as long as he lived.

CHAPTER 11

Jordan, who had just recovered from another of his regular bouts of coughing, looked up with watery eyes and Anders said: "Why don't you see a doctor, Jim? Take a rest?"

"You might make the abduction charge stick," said Jordan as if he hadn't heard him, "in which case he'll get about three years less remission, and then come out and do it again. Somehow we've got to nail him on the other charges. There's nothing more on the Murray girl, I suppose?"

"Not a thing."

"I'm going to see what I can get out of this Mrs. Stringer and her husband. Will you come with me instead of one of my officers?"

"I was going to suggest it. But we'll have to tread softly. Apart from the coincidence of their association and her husband's car being a green Austin with an "H" and a three in the number, we've damn all to go on. She says Mellish has never been in it and there's nothing between them—and we can't prove otherwise."

But Jordan was no more successful with Mavis Stringer than Anders had been. Less in fact because the lapse of time

111

had enabled her to compose herself and even show a degree of acting ability she had never realized that she possessed. After a number of searching questions thrown from different angles, she looked at them with an expression suggesting that, while not annoyed, she had humoured them long enough. "I'm sorry I can't help you. But why do you keep on at me? Are you trying to say that I'm deliberately protecting him?"

"I hope for your sake you're not," said Jordan.

"I've told you all I know, which is nothing, and I'd rather you didn't come here again. I'm sorry and I sincerely hope you catch whoever has done these horrible things and, if it is Peter Mellish, I hope you convict him and he gets what he deserves."

They left her then and Anders, remembering the first interview, said: "She didn't fool me. Her husband comes back today. We'll have someone watching and we'll catch him on his own."

Lewis Wynn listened to Mellish's account of the identification and, when he had taken a statement from him, he decided not to raise any immediate protest.

He was present when Mellish was formally charged with the abduction and pleaded not guilty, and then he left.

Secrecy had been maintained as far as possible but the activity and change of tempo couldn't be disguised from the Press who suddenly appeared like flies and hung around with their usual tenacious patience.

At six o'clock Anders gathered them together at the Murder Headquarters. "Gentlemen," he said, "this afternoon a man has been charged with the abduction of Peggy Finney on the 5th June this year. He is in custody and will appear in court for remand tomorrow morning at ten-thirty."

"What about the Coolidge murders? Can we anticipate further charges, Mr. Anders?"

"I am not at liberty to say. But I do ask for your cooperation in preventing the spread of sensational news. Apart from the legal aspect, there are many people who might be hurt by it.

As soon as possible I will keep you informed of any further details."

They filed out and hurried for the nearest telephones.

But, even with the co-operation of the Press, Anders had been wasting his time. The news spread, and people in Forebridge who came from the seclusion of their homes to talk over garden fences and at street doors, waited eagerly for the confirmation which later appeared in the stop press and on radio and television news.

The infection also spread rapidly to Coolidge where naturally it became more intense. That night the pubs were full and one individual who suggested that they might have got the wrong man was roughly handled.

By seven o'clock Joe Murray was one of the few who hadn't heard about it. His wife, who had been near a complete breakdown, was staying in Devon with his sister, a former nurse, and he sat alone in his mental retreat. He knew he was being a fool to himself, dwelling on it continuously, but it was as if some hidden masochistic force were driving him to suffer so that he could face the worst and be damned to it. For long periods he would linger in her room, touching her things, reading her school notebooks.

The previous day his sister had telephoned. "Joe! It's about Joyce. No, nothing's happened. She just wants to go home. I think she can cope now and she's concerned about you. Will you be there tomorrow? Good. She should arrive early in the evening. Hang on! I'll get her."

Then his wife's slightly husky voice. "Are you all right, Joe?"

"Yes. So you'll be back tomorrow?" He couldn't bring himself to ask her if she were feeling better.

"Yes, Joe. How have you been managing about food... and laundry?"

"I've been all right. I've had a few meals next door. Anyway, I'll stay home tomorrow so I'll be in when you get here. Ring me from the station and I'll come and get you..."

Afterwards he had analysed his feelings. The truth was that, until it was all over, he would rather be on his own. For the time being Joyce had become a side issue and he could not allow himself to worry about her.

Even now he had to remind himself that she could be home any minute, that he was waiting for the phone call from the station.

The phone rang and he automatically felt for his car keys as he answered it. But it was Tom Purdy. "Hallo, Joe. I'm just calling to find out how you are and if there's anything I can do."

"Thanks, but there's nothing really. I thought it was Joyce. She'll be home any time now and is ringing from the station."

"I won't hog the line then. But there's one thing before you go. Have you heard about the chap they've arrested?"

Murray's eyes narrowed. "No."

"It's the one whose made-up pictures have been in the papers for abducting that kid. They've charged him."

When Murray didn't answer, Purdy said: "Are you still there?"

"Yes, I'm here. I hadn't heard. Thanks for telling me."

"I'll ring off then. I don't want to push it but come down whenever you feel like it."

"Thanks again."

He had hardly put the phone down when the key grated in the lock of the front door and then his wife was standing inside, looking into her purse, and a taxi driver was putting her cases in the hall. When she had paid the driver and shut the door, she turned with a nervous smile. "I couldn't get to the phone, and the taxi was there."

Then she ran to him and sobbed on his shoulder and, as his compassion for her grew, an almost unbelievable hatred burned reason away. His jaws were aching before he realized how long and how hard he had been clenching his teeth. He knew now more than ever what he had to do. It would be difficult but he would find a way—once he was sure.

* * *

George Stringer paid off his taxi and lugged his case up the front drive, noting that his wife's Renault was missing from its standing place in front of the garage.

He let himself in and, leaving the case in the hall, wandered through into the main sitting-room. Propped together on the mantelpiece were three letters for him but he merely glanced at them and then went out into the kitchen. There was a savoury smell of something cooking and a note on the gas stove. "Have left a casserole for you."

He turned off the oven, went into the sitting-room and poured himself a drink.

Further up the road, the officer in the small saloon picked up the microphone and got through to Murder Headquarters.

"He's just come in. She hasn't come back yet."

Within ten minutes Anders and Jordan were ringing the front door bell and, as soon as Stringer appeared, something about him evoked an immediate sympathy in Anders. He introduced himself and Jordan and they went inside.

Stringer, obviously curious, said: "Take a seat."

"I believe my officers called the other day during routine enquiries about the abduction of a child?" said Anders.

"That's right. I'd just got back from town and there was a form they asked me to check. My wife had given them some information, mainly about my car."

"You've been at a conference for a few days, I believe?"

"Only two days. I've only just got back."

"Does the name Peter Mellish mean anything to you?"

Stringer slowly shook his head. "No."

"Some time ago he re-tiled your bathroom. Didn't you meet him then?"

"Was he the one who did it? I left all the arrangements to my wife. In the morning I had always gone before he arrived and he was gone before I got back. I never saw him."

"Did you know he helped your wife to buy her car recently?"

They saw him stiffen and for a moment he stared into space. Then he cleared his throat. "No, I didn't know."

"She bought the car on the 6th June. Up to that time she drove yours. Were there any restrictions on her use of it?"

"None whatever."

"So it was mainly her car?"

"I didn't use it much, only very occasionally at weekends. In fact I'm not much of a driver."

"Do you know why she bought herself a car then, an inferior one to yours, and put herself to unnecessary expense?"

"No, I . . ."

"You didn't alter the arrangements, tell her she couldn't drive it after that time?"

"Of course not."

"I'm sorry to ask this question, but is there some trouble between you and your wife?"

Stringer got up from his chair and went over to the fireplace. With his back to them he said quietly: "Yes, there is, but I can't see it's any concern of yours."

"Mr. Stringer," said Jordan, "we wouldn't be asking if it weren't. Mr. Anders and I don't get any joy out of prying into your personal affairs. Has your wife been in touch with you since you've been away?"

"No."

"Is another man involved in this trouble between you?"

"I'd rather not say any more about it," said Stringer, sitting down again.

Jordan coughed once or twice and then, with some impatience, said: "Much as we'd rather not ask it, it's got to be answered. We are on one of the most serious murder enquiries this country has seen. I'll ask you again. Is another man involved in your trouble?"

There was a long pause and then Stringer said in a low voice: "Yes."

"Who is this man?"

"That I don't know. I don't know. She wouldn't tell me."

Anders and Jordan exchanged glances. "Do you know if this man has been in your car?" asked Anders.

"No," said Stringer rather too emphatically.

116

"Have you seen the evening paper or heard the radio news?"

"No."

"Then you are not aware that Peter Mellish has been arrested and charged with the abduction of a child?"

The colour drained from Stringer's face and then slowly returned. "I didn't know that. But what has it to do with my wife and my car?"

"We think it possible that Peter Mellish is the man involved with your wife, that he used your car during this offence and also to commit the murders in Coolidge."

This time Stringer gazed at them in open astonishment. "My car? Mavis? That's quite ridiculous."

"We're not suggesting that your wife is aware that the car has been used for this purpose, but we should like to take it away for examination."

"Look here, have you asked my wife about this?"

"Oh yes."

"What does she say? Does she say that this... Mellish is the man she's involved with?"

"She didn't say she was involved with anyone."

"Did she say she knew him?"

"Yes, and she admits that he helped her buy her car."

"That's the only reason why you want to take my car?"

"The only one we can give you at the moment."

"I'm not doing it, unless you have a warrant. Not until I've seen my wife anyway. People will get to know. What will it look like?"

"Now, Mr. Stringer," said Anders, but it was no use. The more they tried to persuade him, the more obstinate he seemed to become.

"Very well," said Jordan. "I hope you know what you're doing. I expect we'll be back."

The hall clock had already struck midnight when Mavis Stringer got home. The house was very quiet. When she went into the kitchen and switched on the light, she saw that her

117

note had been moved to the table but the casserole was still in the oven untouched.

Ever since that night, George had slept in one of the guest rooms and she saw that the door was closed. In her own room she undressed and for a few moments surveyed herself in front of the mirror, thinking and thinking.

She was in bed and about to turn out the light when George came in. His hair was untidy and he had put on his dressing-gown hurriedly, for it was caught up at the back, making him look rather ridiculous.

"You didn't eat anything," she said.

He stood near the end of the bed. "The police came to see me this evening."

She lay back with her head on the pillow and refused to look at him or comment.

"I understand they have already seen you again?"

"They came yesterday morning."

"What did you tell them?"

"There wasn't anything to tell. Your car is something like the one this awful man used and they wanted to know if anybody besides you or me had driven it. What did they want with you?"

"Mavis, please! Tell me the truth. Is he the man, the one who was in the car with you, this man named Mellish?"

She gave an unconvincing laugh. "Don't be absurd. He's the man who did our tiling."

"I know that. He also helped you about buying your car."

"They told you that?" she asked after a pause.

"Yes. You admitted it to them."

He began pacing the room and when he spoke again his voice had lost its calm. "For God's sake, Mavis, what is happening to you? You're not telling the truth. Things come back to me now. He *is* the man. I don't know if he's ever driven the car but he's been in it. Now he's been charged with abducting this child." He covered his face with his hands. "What have you got yourself mixed up in? Oh, God, this is terrible! The police aren't fools; they'll find out what they what to know."

She sat up, her self-control shaken by his sudden outburst. "I *will* tell you. Yes, I *will* tell you. And this is the truth. It was Peter Mellish with me in the car that day. And this is also the truth. He was with me all the afternoon so he couldn't have had anything to do with Angela Murray. That's what they're after, because he looks something like the picture. But it couldn't have been him, and our car has nothing to do with it."

Although he had guessed it, the emphatic admission came as a shock. Eventually he said: "Why didn't you tell the police this? Wouldn't it clear him?"

"Would they believe me, when they found how . . . how it was with us? He had nothing to do with this other child either, so they won't prove it. But if I tell them he's been in the car they'll keep on and on."

"I can't see your reasoning."

"And, if you want to know, I was also thinking of you."

"I wish I could believe that."

"Why do you put up with me now, George?"

"That's a good question! But my words the other day must have been prophetic. You're going to need me in the end, more than you'll need him."

Then he went back to his room.

CHAPTER 12

The next morning it rained, but not heavily enough to keep away the crowd which gathered outside Forebridge courthouse. The arrival of the blue police van used for conveying prisoners was greeted by the frightening growl of the potential lynch mob, and as it edged into the court precincts angry shouts followed it on its way. But the van was a decoy and Mellish, with a coat over his head, was being smuggled from a police car into a side entrance.

Inside the court the magistrate heard a brief résumé of the case and evidence of arrest from Anders. Mellish was remanded in custody of seven days and as he was escorted to the prison remand centre, Jordan returned to Coolidge to continue the re-evaluation of the mass of information which had accumulated since he had been there, in the hope of finding something which had previously meant nothing to them.

It was mid-afternoon when a detective-sergeant produced the questionnaire which aroused Jordan's interest.

After the second murder, a Mrs. Gascoigne had been crossing the road from her car when she had been nearly run over by a car traveling westward at a fast speed. She admitted that it was mainly her fault and that she had caused the driver to swerve and brake. The driver, a man, had skidded across the road as he had gone past her and had glanced back at her and had shaken his fist before driving off. The spot was a little over five miles from where the body had been found and on a route which could have led from it. About half an hour later she thought she saw the man again in the same car in Coolidge, but this time a woman was driving. She had no idea of the number of the car. It could have been green or blue, or greeny-blue, but she wasn't very good at remembering detail. It was a saloon car, she knew that. She couldn't describe the woman but the man, she thought, was dark and she might recognize his face again. It was on the day the murder had been committed and on the day and covering the time when Mavis Stringer went to her hairdresser in Byfleet on the outskirts of Coolidge.

"Go and see her and ask her if she will be good enough to accompany you here," said Jordan.

Meanwhile Carver was having second thoughts about their search of 113 Cluny Avenue.

Mellish's notebook had been extremely useful. They had traced his contacts mentioned in it and these had led to others.

Scores of people had been seen and most of them had expressed amazement. They had admitted—sometimes under pressure—payments made to him and it soon became obvious that Mellish should be quite comfortably off. He was unknown to the income tax and employment authorities, and he was on no doctor's panel. As far as could be ascertained he had no connection with any form of officialdom.

Search as they might, they could find no bank books, business references, safe deposit keys, left luggage tickets or any indication where he might have deposited money. He didn't gamble. They knew he had been abroad but there was no passport or seaman's ticket. In fact there was nothing to show that he had ever existed.

There was no evidence that he and his mother lived in some

luxury since he'd been home. Neighbours now eagerly volunteered information. She was now never, as she used to be, short of a pound and she obviously spent quite a lot on clothes, even if they were sometimes in poor taste. They knew of her addiction to bingo. She was also a regular at the Bull and gin and tonics weren't cheap anywhere.

What, thought Carver, had he done with his money? He wouldn't have put it where he couldn't get at it, or where his mother could.

Hudson found the answer during another visit to the house. The built-in wardrobe in Mellish's bedroom had a false bottom and when this was lifted it revealed a tray-like compartment stacked with currency notes.

There was an envelope with a passport, a seaman's ticket and sundry papers. And there was another, larger envelope. This contained a number of coloured photographs depicting acts of sexual and sadistic depravity that put them in a class by themselves.

With time to dwell on the situation a slight dent had appeared in Mellish's confidence and his confinement had affected him more than he had anticipated. While he had been in the police cell it hadn't concerned him over much, but his reception into the prison remand block had irritated him and had also emphasized the formidable nature of the forces ranged against him. The attitude towards him of contemptuous superiority had been evident from the beginning and when, soon after he had arrived, they had insisted on his taking a bath rather than allowing him the option, the indignity had struck home.

Wynn's attitude when he had called to see him hadn't altogether pleased him either. "Whatever you told the police, I want the truth if I'm going to do any good. This identification may or may not stand up but, if it does, it could make all the difference."

"From what I've read, the evidence of one witness identifying someone doesn't carry much weight. It wasn't me she saw, that's for certain, and you ought to be able to get around her."

"But what about this business of changing the cylinder head gasket on your car? They've impounded it now so they must be confident you didn't work on that."

Mellish had given thought to this. "I was a bit of a fool there. I didn't."

"You admit that? *Now* you admit it?"

"Being innocent, I never dreamed it would be necessary. They were going round to everybody and I got narked at their questions. I *was* going to change it. There was a bit of a blow, I reckoned, but I did one of the wheel bearings first—rear offside. That's what I did actually."

Slowly Wynn opened his briefcase, extracted a pad of paper and took out his pen. "You now say you didn't change the gasket and you told them you had because you were irritated and didn't think it mattered?"

"That's right."

Wynn wrote it down. "In fact you put in new wheel bearings? In which wheel?"

"Rear offside."

"Is there anything else you haven't told me because you didn't think it mattered?"

"No."

"Are you sure you haven't been seeing Mrs. Stringer?"

"If you don't believe me, ask her. I can't see what she's got to do with it anyway."

"Only the fact that up to the day after the abduction she'd been driving the right type of car and then you helped her buy a different sort of car for herself."

"There are hundreds of cars like her old man's. Do you mean to tell me they can make something of that?"

"Not on what they've got so far." Wynn looked at him with some calculation. "I expect they'll ask for another remand. When it comes to the committal proceedings I'll apply for legal aid. How much can you go to if necessary?"

"There's about two thousand quid available but I don't see why I should use that."

"We'll see. I'm glad we've cleared up the car angle. That's something."

"About two thousand pounds," he'd said, but the next day he received another unpleasant surprise. A warder opened the door and Anders and Jordan walked in. When the door had been shut behind them. Anders put a Gladstone-type bag on the bench seat. "Good morning, Mr. Mellish. Just one or two questions. You know the caution? You needn't say anything unless you wish to do so, and so on." He paused and then said: "How much money do you reckon you had in your hiding-place in the wardrobe?"

Mellish was on his feet before he realized it, his face flushed with anger. "What d'you mean? You'd no bloody right!"

"Calm down. You'd be surprised what rights we have when necessary."

His fists clenched, Mellish slowly sat down again. He mustn't get rattled so that he forgot when he was saying!

"Well, how much?" Anders repeated.

"I'm answering no questions."

"I'll tell you. There were two thousand, one hundred and forty-nine pounds." Anders went to his case, took out a large envelope and extracted the mounted photographs. "When and where did you take these?"

Mellish barely looked at them. "I'm not answering questions."

"You admit they are yours and were with the money?"

"No questions. D'you mind going? I'll say it all in court."

"Mr. Jordan wants a word with you."

"Bollocks to Mr. Jordan!" said Mellish, and then regretted his uncharacteristic lapse into the vernacular. It was a sign that he might be weakening.

Jordan made an entry in his notebook. "The caution still stands," he said. "Now, on the 6th April a witness saw a man of your description driving a car of a similar type to Mrs.

124

Stringer's near Coolidge. It nearly ran her down. Shortly after she again saw the man in the same car in Coolidge with a woman. This time the woman was driving. Would you consent to be put up for identification?"

He looked at them with scorn and decided that, if he said anything at all, he would pick his words carefully.

"I've already had a taste of your methods. I'm innocent but because one or two things fit in with your ideas you're going to do your bloody best to make it stick. You can put all this down and let everybody know. It's been going on too long, hasn't it? Well, I can tell them what they've done. They've at last got someone, doesn't matter whether he did it, so long as they can cook up enough. They want a body so that they can write it off and save their faces. Now, get out and leave me alone!"

When they had gone, Mellish paced his cell for some time. For years uninterrupted success had made him feel invincible, almost super-invincible. He'd been clever, never leaving a trace, always backing things both ways. He'd even considered the possibility of being interrogated and he'd studied the methods and listened to the advice of boastful old lags. Say nothing and they can do nothing! But it wasn't quite so easy, and for the first time he looked to the future and possible means of escape.

CHAPTER 13

George Stringer had been on Tom Purdy's conscience. They hadn't met since the night of the first search for Angela Murray and, although he had telephoned without success a couple of times, he had since let it slide.

Driving past the house on the Sunday afternoon, he saw Stringer at one of the front windows and acting on impulse he stopped and backed up to the gate. At first he hesitated. Mavis could be at home and he wasn't anxious to see her again yet awhile. On the other hand he knew George was there, and as he was right outside he might as well chance it.

He got out and sauntered up the front path, feeling something like a conspirator who has rather been left out of things.

Stringer opened the door and said: "Oh, hallo, Tom!" and Purdy couldn't decide whether he was reluctant to see him or just couldn't care less.

"Hallo, George! Meant to see you before this. Mavis home?"

"No. Come on in."

Stringer led him into the room at the front of the house and Purdy, sensing a certain awkwardness in his manner, decided to come out with it. "Been worried about you, George. Rang a couple of times. What happened after?"

"Nothing."

"Hell, man, you looked dreadful at the time. It was none of my business but ... I wondered if ... You know ... If I could be of any help ..."

"You haven't mentioned it to anybody else?"

"Good lord, no! Did you find out who the bloke was?"

"No. In fact I'm trying to forget about it."

Purdy looked at him with some surprise and then shrugged. "Sorry! I thought ... you might need someone to talk to about it. Sorry!"

"Don't get me wrong. You couldn't have known and I do appreciate your motives. Only it's rather a delicate matter. Here, it's a bit too early for a drink but would you like some tea?"

"Yes. Yes, perhaps I would."

"Come on out with me then while I make it."

But Stringer only got as far as the door when the bell rang. Purdy waited just inside the room. A man's voice said: "Good afternoon, Mr. Stringer," and almost immediately Stringer put his head into the room. "Sorry about this," he said. "Shan't be long," and he shut the door.

Purdy strolled to the window. The sound of mumbled voices receded and he saw that Stringer and a tall man in a dark grey suit were walking towards the garage. Stringer seemed to be protesting but after the tall man had produced a sheet of paper he opened the garage.

Purdy had never been anxious to pry into other people's affairs but in this case he couldn't help himself. He moved behind the curtain to see another man appear from somewhere. Within a few minutes Stringer's car nosed out of the garage, rolled down the drive on to the road and sped away.

The tall man said something and then left. Outside a car door slammed and an engine started up. When Purdy saw Stringer returning to the house, he moved to a chair away from the window and sat with one leg crossed over the other.

But it was several minutes before Stringer came in and something had obviously shaken him.

"I'm sorry about that," he said. "I won't be able to ask you to stop after all. I've got to go out."

"That's all right," said Purdy, getting up. "Give me a ring some time. I'll leave it to you."

He drove away, intrigued and sorry he couldn't help. Unless he was mistaken, George Stringer was in some sort of trouble. It was more the look on his face than what had happened.

And Stringer himself was wondering what else they had found out to enable them to get a warrant. He wandered aimlessly about the house and then sat with his head in his hands. "God! Oh, God! What am I going to do?"

For days Mavis Stringer had lived on her nerves and the skilful use of make-up couldn't completely hide the shadows under her eyes and the drawn look on her face. Then, as if nature had switched on a protective mechanism, she had retreated into a sort of steel-lined mental vacuum which protected her against thoughts of dread and despair.

Her concern became not for next year, next week or next day, but for no more than the following hour: what she might do with it, where she might go, who if anybody at all she might be with. Like a computer, her mind had become programmed, with Mellish at the centre of things, and her reaction to any challenge was automatic and unemotional.

When Anders had called for the car to be taken away she had again been with Helen Reeves, a well-meaning but singularly unattractive person, too flattered to wonder why she had suddenly become so popular with a friend of long standing but limited and infrequent association. She didn't realize — and neither did Mavis consciously — that her naïveté and unenquiring mind were perfectly suited to the occasion. She talked, boringly most of the time, and Mavis only half listened and was able to relax, and she was made a fuss of.

In the hope and expectation that George would be in bed, Mavis left it late before she returned home. But he was waiting

128

in the sitting-room, the single standard lamp throwing up the shiny vermilion on one side of his dressing-gown and the deepening lines on his face.

At first he said nothing but when his whole body seemed to tense she had a sudden fear that he might become violent. Then he spoke in a hollow, flat voice. "They have taken the car for examination."

"What for?"

"Are you really telling me you don't know?"

"No, I don't know."

"I couldn't stop them taking it. They had a warrant and they must have a good reason for getting that." His voice rose and crackled with emotion. "Why don't you tell me, so I know what to do?"

"There's nothing to tell. I'm going to bed."

As she went to pass him, he grabbed her arm, but it was more a pleading gesture than an angry one and it somehow irritated her. She shook herself free and went upstairs, calm again as she remembered how thoroughly she had cleaned every mark from the car.

The complete absence of prints on the metal work of the car was disappointing to Jordan and Anders, but it told them something. Someone had gone to great pains to clean it and, as on Stringer's admission it hadn't been driven since the day Peggy Finney had been abducted, it seemed more than a little significant.

At Forensic, a specially-designed and powerful vacuum with a spotless white bag had sucked every loose particle from the inside of the car. The bag had been emptied on to a white, fine-textured cloth completely free from any foreign matter, and the painstaking examination had begun.

Two possibly exhibits had emerged: a fairly long auburn hair similar in texture and composition to that on the head of one of the murdered children, and a small quantity of soil, similar in composition to that prevalent at the spot where the victim had been found.

"Two more links in the chain, but not enough," said Jordan.

Anders lit his pipe and blew a cloud of smoke thoughtfully at the ceiling. "There's one thing I don't like about it. This cleaning of the car suggests collusion by Mrs. Stringer. She didn't strike me as a woman with homicidal or sadistic tendencies."

"She's protecting him but she's doing it because she's blind and won't believe he's guilty. We've seen it often enough before."

"I think it's about time we tried some shock treatment, and we can do it when we return the car."

They made sure that Mavis Stringer was alone in the house when they took the car back. At once Anders sensed a subtle change in her. She unlocked the garage and when they had put the car away, she said: "I hope you're satisfied now?"

Jordan looked at her as if he knew more than he cared to divulge. "Not quite," he said. "Do you mind if we come inside for a few minutes?"

"Again? What is it now?"

"After you, Mrs. Stringer."

She seemed on the point of refusing and then, with tightened lips, she led them inside but no further than the hall. Anders shut the front door.

"I believe it is true to say that neither you nor your husband has driven the car since the 5th June?" said Jordan.

"If that's the day before I got my own car, I haven't driven it."

"Who usually cleans the car?"

"My husband. Sometimes we go to the car-wash."

"He says he hasn't been near it since."

"He probably hasn't then."

"Who cleaned it the last time, very thoroughly I might say?"

Her top teeth rubbed over her bottom lip. "I did and, if you want to know why, it was because I didn't want him throwing it up at me that I'd left it dirty after I'd finished with it."

"And why did you finish with it?"

130

"That's personal." She hesitated. "But I expect you already know. We had a row."

"A row over your association with Peter Mellish?"

"It had nothing to do with him and it has nothing to do with you either."

Anders opened his case and took out two of the more repellent of Mellish's photographs. "I don't like to do this, Mrs. Stringer, but would you look at these?"

She was visibly shaken. Then she stared at him indignantly. "How dare you show me such disgusting things? How dare you? I shall complain about this."

"They belong to Peter Mellish. They were found in his room and it is quite possible that he took them himself."

"I don't believe you. I think this is just a trick of yours to make me say something which isn't true."

"Come now, Mrs. Stringer!"

"Please go. Let yourselves out," she said and went into a room and slammed the door.

"He must have one hell of a hold on her," said Anders as they drove away. "Surely she can't be all that blind?"

Jordan gave a grunt. "Don't believe it. The trick-cyclists have got a name for it but it happens all right. The only thing that's likely to do any good is if it's personal against her. If he left her or carried on with somebody else for instance!"

Among many of the citizens of Forebridge and Coolidge relief had been partly replaced by a smouldering anger. If Mellish had been suddenly released in their midst he almost certainly wouldn't have seen the following day.

But after the second remand an uneasy doubt was added. Why had there yet been no mention of a murder charge? What was happening? Persistent questions from the Press had resulted in a mollifying but indecisive announcement. "The police have again interviewed a man concerning the murders at Coolidge."

In most gatherings the subject was raised sooner or later: the horrifying aspect of the crimes, the unending suffering of the parents and thoughts for children who, if the predator went unconvicted, would still be in danger. And in the locals, where alcohol drove passions to overcome reason, violence simmered not far below the surface.

Lenny Myall, who had been warned that on no account should he disclose anything concerning the nature of his evidence, had held out for some time. But the feeling of privilege and power during such a momentous occasion was difficult to hide. The knowing hint escaped before he realized it and the knowing look was there all the time.

In the end he told his wife. ". . . but for Christ sake, keep it to yourself, Phoeb. This is bloody dynamite but I reckon I ought to be able to tell my own missus."

In a few days it had got around. The saloon lounge said a woman, a female, was involved; in the public bar, some dame, tart or bitch. And somehow it returned full circle to Myall who, when cornered by large and hostile associates, admitted some of the circumstances but sought refuge in the lie that he'd no idea who the woman was.

Jordan and Anders were also a little disturbed, Jordan the more so, although they both felt that the evidence had to come sooner or later. But, and this created the urgency, it would be tremendously more difficult if, by some chance, Mellish were acquitted of the abduction charge before the murder charge could be made. Evidence for the Coolidge murders which might be insufficient in itself could, if supported by evidence for the abduction, be formidable. Apart from a few inconclusive items, there was not one shred of scientific evidence. There was no direct evidence. But if it could be proved beyond doubt that Mellish had been in Coolidge during the material time, had access to and was driving a suspect car during those times, then, with the identification, if it stood, of Mrs. Conway and Mellish's own evasions, any defence could be in trouble.

The key to these hopes was Mrs. Stringer but so far she hadn't budged and they could not lawfully put any pressure on her.

But Tom Purdy had been thinking. The man he had seen outside George Stringer's house? Recognition had come suddenly. Of course he'd seen his picture in the papers and when he'd been interviewed on television. He was the detective in charge of the search and this latest business. They'd taken George's car. It was a green Austin 1800, the same as they'd been looking for. But they couldn't suspect George, not George! Then he remembered that a man was already in custody and, in any case, George hardly ever drove. It was a standing joke, George's reluctance to drive. How he had ever passed the test was a perpetual wonder. And George not wanting to talk about the bloke in the car with Mavis—did that mean something?

For several days he chewed it over until, like a heated gas, it threatened to explode. Harry Bristow provided the natural outlet. Purdy rang him just about seven when he thought he might be at home. Bristow was at home and, by his clogged and indistinct speech, in the middle of his dinner.

"I'm going to the Samaritan this evening, Harry," said Purdy. "Thought I might see you there?"

"I don't know." Bristow cleared his throat and Purdy heard him call out: "You want to do anything tonight, Paula?" and a voice in the background said: "No, why?"

Bristow's voice came through normally again, minus the effect of a mouthful of food. "OK. What's on?"

"Nothing. I just wanted a chat."

"What time?"

"About half eight?"

"See you there!"

When Bristow arrived, Purdy had his pint of mild waiting for him. Bristow never deviated. They retired to a table in the corner. "Cheers!"

"Cheers!" said Bristow and Purdy watched him, fascinated, as over half the beer disappeared down his throat as if it were being swept down a wide drainpipe. Bristow lowered his glass and relaxed with a sigh. "Well, how's things?"

"All right. And you? No more domestic strife?"

"No, ever since the business of poor old Joe's kid. But I've thought a lot about it, Tom. Stood outside myself and all that. I'm not so bloody marvellous."

"Who is?"

"Looking back, I wonder what you blokes must have thought of me sometimes, let alone Paula."

"I don't get you."

"You bloody well do! What about the night I upset old Farmer? Got all stewed up over nothing and shouted the odds. I'm always doing it, or was. Too bloody big-headed and inclined to hit the roof."

"That's nothing. We all had a laugh afterwards."

"But suppose you had to live with it? See it from Paula's angle. Now I count up to ten and when I find I'm in the middle of a wind-up I stop and even apologize sometimes. You'd be surprised how it's changed her too."

"Glad things are all right now. But you mentioned Joe's kid. Do you know anything about this chap they've got in custody?"

"Only that he's called Mellish and lives on the estate. His mother's in hospital, I believe. Best place for her."

Purdy toyed with his glass. "You remember what we discussed about Mavis Stringer?"

"About her being with this bloke in the car?"

"That's right. Well, the other day I called to see George," said Purdy, and he told Bristow what had happened.

Bristow took a swig at his remaining beer. "You reckon then that George is in some sort of trouble?"

"Not so much George."

"Who then, Mavis?"

"I don't know. But who normally drives the car?"

Bristow gave a grunting laugh. "Not George."

"Remembering that George's car is like the one they've been after, why should they take it away?"

"Christ! Because they think it might be *the* car?"

"I can't imagine any other reason."

"But what've George and Mavis got to do with it?"

"Mavis has been hitting it off with another bloke, hasn't she? Is she likely to be carrying on with more than one?"

"Shouldn't think so."

"Suppose this bloke is the one they've got inside? It sort of ties up, doesn't it?"

Bristow stood up. "Finish your drink," he said, and, after Purdy had emptied his glass, went to the bar for a refill. When he returned, Purdy said: "Another thing, Mavis hasn't been around lately, ever since in fact."

"D'you reckon the police know she's been carrying on with this bloke and have put two and two together?"

"What *have* they put together?"

Bristow's heavy forehead wrinkled so that he resembled a puzzled mastiff. "There's been no mention of this chap being charged with the murders yet, has there?"

"Not to my knowledge."

"I'll tell you what, there's been talk of a woman being involved. I don't like the sound of it."

For a short while they sat in silence and then Purdy said: "But she can't know about it, can she? Perhaps he took the car without her knowing."

"What—every time?"

"Maybe not. We're not sure he always used the same car, are we? It could be that the police have traced the car and found the bloke, but they can't tie the two together. How can we be sure they know Mavis has been curling up with somebody else?"

"It's possible but I still can't see it. If the two of them were on that basis, she'd have known if he'd used the car and she'd have told them, wouldn't she?"

Bristow clenched his fist and his jaw hardened. "When you think of those poor little kids and then poor old Joe's kid still missing, it gets right inside you. Talk about the bloody death penalty, they ought to chuck him to the crowd, the evil, sodding bastard! And if anybody's helping him, they ought to go with him."

"I can't believe that Mavis would . . . No, I can't believe that."

"There's one way of finding out," said Bristow, putting both hands on the table and becoming tense. "Go to the police and tell them what you saw."

"Steady on. I can't do that."

"Why not?"

"Well, I can't. Probably nothing in it, and don't you think George would have told them if it were necessary? He saw them too, you know."

"So what?" Bristow was almost shouting now and one or two people looked across from the other side of the bar. "If he's told them, it won't matter if you tell them again, will it?"

"Keep your voice down," said Purdy, looking anxiously over his shoulder.

Bristow thrust his head forward. "All right," he said in an aggressive whisper, "if you don't tell them, I will. And then they'll come round asking questions. How would that suit you, eh?"

"I can't see . . . Be sensible!"

"I mean it, Tom."

They stared at each other, Bristow like an enraged lion and Purdy a trapped stag. "Well, tomorrow I'll . . ."

"Never mind tomorrow," said Bristow. "Finish up and we'll do it now."

Outside the police station Purdy hesitated. With his indecision gone, he felt himself resenting Bristow's bull-like insistence, although he conceded the motive.

"All right, Harry. All right. Now we're here, I don't need you to hold my hand, and you can't contribute anything."

"You *are* going to tell them? You're not going to enquire about a missing dog or something?"

"I thought you said you'd changed?"

Bristow grunted. "All right, but you might give me a ring to tell me what happened."

"I'll do that. I'm not stopping you from waiting outside but I don't know how long I'll be, do I?"

"OK. Give me a ring then!"

The constable at the desk eyed Purdy with cautious respect. People called at police stations for a variety of reasons: lost and found property, production of driving documents, even confessions of crime. Then there were the nuts with secret information! Only two months ago a smartly-dressed, rather effeminate-looking young man had appeared and exultantly claimed, subsequently proved true, that he had half killed his father-in-law. With four years' service behind him, he had learned that the degree of apparent respectability meant little. You started from square one, every time.

"Good evening, sir?"

"Good evening. Er . . . I'd like . . . er . . . to see the officer in charge of the murders . . . and the man in custody."

The caution deepened. "I see, sir. And the name?"

"Purdy. Tom Purdy."

After a whispered conversation with a sergeant who appeared from the back, the constable made a call on the telephone. Then he moved along the counter towards Purdy. "If you'll take a seat, sir, somebody will be over shortly."

Purdy sat on a seat against the wall, conflicting loyalties to Stringer and public duty giving him a queasy stomach.

A man with a mop of curly hair and thick suède shoes came in and belligerently produced some documents to the constable. Two girls and a dog followed shortly after, and waited. Then a tall man with wide sloping shoulders, who looked as if he could be twice as nasty as Bristow if he wanted to, came through the door and his eyes immediately alighted on Purdy. "Mr. Purdy?" he asked.

"Yes," said Purdy, getting up, and the tall man led him into a room at the back.

"I'm Detective Chief Inspector Carver. I understand you've got something to tell me?"

"Well, yes, I don't know whether it's got anything to do with it, and if it hasn't I'll be sorry I came here."

"Let's find out, shall we? And we may as well sit down."

"I believe you took George Stringer's car away the other day?"

"Did we?"

"You did, didn't you?"

"Go on, Mr. Purdy. You were supposed to be telling me something."

"I was in Mr. Stringer's house when it happened and I saw it through the window. There was a policeman, it wasn't you but I've seen his picture in the papers. The car was driven away and George seemed a bit upset when they'd gone." Purdy hesitated but Carver didn't interrupt. "Mavis, his wife, drives the car mostly and the night we went on the search for Angela Murray—that's not long after she was reported missing— George came with me in my car and we went down the old quarry. Look, I don't want to say any more unless there's some point."

"Mr. Purdy, we'll be very interested in anything you can tell us about the Stringers and their car, very interested indeed."

"Well, I parked the car and we walked across to look behind some bushes—and there they were, having it off in George's car, Mavis and some bloke."

"Yes?"

"Is that . . . er . . . any help?" said Purdy lamely.

"Do you know who the man is?"

"Never seen him before."

"Does Mr. Stringer?"

"No, so he says. At the time he took one look, went sort of green and walked all the way back home."

"And you've seen him since then and he still doesn't know who the man is?"

"So he says. Says he wants to forget about it."

"Would you recognize the man again?"

"Don't think so. He was on top and I only got a back view. I'd say he was a well-built fellow with thick, dark hair."

"I'm very grateful to you for coming forward. Would you

now come with me to Murder Headquarters where we'll go into this in more detail?"

An hour later, feeling as if he'd been through an extremely exhausting aptitude test, Purdy prepared to go home. Anders had come in half way through and by the time they'd finished they had drained him of all the information he was able to give about the Stringers and the Murrays.

CHAPTER 14

Within minutes of George Stringer leaving for his office, they called at the house. The policewoman waited in the car.

When Mavis Stringer opened the door Anders said: "Good morning, Mrs. Stringer. We would like a few words with you," and with barely a pause he and Jordan went inside. Their manner discouraged protest.

"What is it?"

"I think, if you don't mind, we'll go where you can sit down."

The suggestion of impending shock was not there by accident and, although they had no direct proof yet that Mellish was the man who had been in the car with her, they gave the impression that there was not much they didn't know.

She preceded them into the sitting-room, and when she remained standing Anders pulled a chair forward for her. She sat down.

"You will remember that I asked you if Peter Mellish had ever been in your husband's car with you?"

She stared woodenly in front of her.

"You remember that, Mrs. Stringer?"

"Do I?"

"You said that he hadn't. In fact several times you insisted that he hadn't. You also said that you hadn't seen him between the time he tiled your bathroom and when you met him and asked him to help you buy a car in the old quarry just outside the town. You were seen and have been identified. Why did you lie about it? Why are you protecting a human monster who murders little children?"

Her head jerked up. "That's a lie. He didn't; I know he didn't."

"Really? Then it's your duty to tell us how and why you know that."

"I admit we were in the car that evening. I'll admit it. But he was with me all the time, all the afternoon as well, so he couldn't have had anything to do with it."

"What time did you meet him?"

"Before three. We went for a ride and had some tea in Freeling. Then we came back and went to the quarry."

"You lied before. Why should we believe you now?"

"Because it's true. It's true, I tell you. The tea shop, we got there about four, someone there could have seen us. Ask them."

"And you were together the whole time?"

"The whole time, so how could he have done it?"

"Why didn't you tell us this before?"

"Because . . . Because it's not something you talk about and I didn't think you'd believe me."

"Is that the only reason?"

She nodded.

"We should have been more likely to believe you if you'd told the truth in the first place." Anders went to the door and signalled to the policewoman, who came in. "Mrs. Stringer is accompanying us to Headquarters to clear up one or two points," said Anders.

Mavis Stringer didn't move but when the policewoman touched her arm she said: "I want to go upstairs first."

Anders nodded at the policewoman. "Go with her."

* * *

141

For over an hour they threatened, pleaded and cajoled but they couldn't shift her and so they left her for a while.

"I think she's telling the truth about this Angela Murray," said Jordan.

"So do I. If she's called by the defence he might get away with the abduction charge as well."

"Mind you, the Murray kid hasn't been found yet and there's no absolute proof she's dead even."

"But everyone's satisfied that she is," said Anders, "and what a red herring for the defence to come up with. He didn't kill her, so who did? We've got to have something really strong to beat that. I don't like it, Jim. We're so near. I feel it, but it could slip away from us. I'm going through the files again."

Anders finished reading the statement by Myall and then he called out to Sergeant Hudson. "Where's Sergeant Gisling?"

"Off duty, sir."

"Fetch him, will you? Wherever he is—have him report to me as soon as possible."

Gisling arrived in under half an hour, a strip of sticking plaster on one side of his face. "Was in the middle of shaving, sir. You want to see me?"

Anders leaned back in his chair with the statement in his hands. "You remember you told me that Myall said that he'd upped the price of Mrs. Stringer's car and that Mellish got fifty pounds out of it?"

"That's right, sir, so he did."

"And that he refused to include it in his statement?"

"He wouldn't put it on paper. Said he'd deny it if we pushed him."

Anders slid the statement on to the desk. "Go and get him!"

"What, now, sir? Suppose he's on his own there?"

"He'll have to shut the place up. But I want him here as soon as possible."

"Right, sir," said Gisling. "He'll come whether he wants to or not."

Myall was far from pleased when he was brought to Head-quarters. "It's a bit thick, guv'nor. What about my business?"

"Sit down and listen to what I've got to say. You won't lose by it in the long run." Anders pushed over his cigarettes and Myall took one and lit it.

"Coffee?" asked Anders.

"How long are we going to be?"

"As quick as possible."

"All right, then."

Anders said "Two" to Hudson at the door and gave his attention to Myall again. "I see there's no mention in your statement of this side deal you had with Mellish?"

"What side deal?"

Anders leaned forward. "I'll tell you something in confidence. One of the most dangerous and despicable killers I've ever known is now in custody here, and without a break on our side he could get away with it. He's a psychopath and he'll do it again and again. I'm working on a hunch and I need your co-operation. We both know what happened between you and Mellish. I want you to write it down in the form of a statement. Mrs. Stringer is here and I want to show the statement to her and I want you to be there to back it up."

Myall started to protest and Anders held up his hand. "Afterwards we'll destroy the statement and you can go back to the first one you made. I want you to do this and if you don't I can tell you now that your life won't be worth living, round here anyway. That's how strongly I feel about it."

Myall faltered for a moment. Then he drew on his cigarette and said: "OK."

Mavis Stringer sat in the small room, ignoring the police-woman who was with her. There was a tightness across her head and her throat felt dry. Silence deepened her depression and noises jarred.

When the door opened she looked down at the floor but she was conscious that the two detectives were there and another, smaller man. Anders's tone had changed considerably.

"Mrs. Stringer, we appreciate what you must be going through and we can help you if you will let us. I believe you've met Mr. Myall before?"

She looked up at Myall, who nodded.

"Yes," she said. "He's the man I bought my car from."

Anders put the statement on her lap. "That is a statement he made. Will you read it?"

She looked down, guardedly at first, and took up the statement. Then, as she read it, her expression altered. Her hand clenched, crumpling the corner of the paper, and suddenly she let it go and covered her face with her hands. "No! It can't be true! He wouldn't!"

Anders looked at Myall, who said: "I'm sorry, missus. It's true all right. It was his idea not mine."

After that the sobs were uncontrollable and it was some time before they could get through to her. Myall left the room with his statement and at the first opportunity Anders said: "Now, please let's have the truth. Did Peter Mellish ever drive your car?"

Dumbly she nodded.

"On his own?"

She nodded again.

"And you will make a statement?"

"Yes. Oh, God, yes! I don't know..."

Jordan moved forward to take over.

George Stringer received the telephone call at his office shortly after he had returned from a lunch he had hardly touched. It was from Anders. "Don't get the wrong impression, but I think, if you possibly can, you should come home."

Fear clutched at Stringer. The wrong impression? What was the wrong impression? "What's happened?"

"We have seen your wife again and she is, well, emotionally upset. The doctor has attended her but there's no real cause for alarm. A policewoman is staying with her until you get there."

"Something's happened?"

"We'll meet you at the railway station and explain. What time will you get in?"

Stringer looked at his watch. "I'm not sure how the trains run in the afternoon. At about four-thirty I should think."

"If for some reason you do get there much earlier, or later, and there's no one waiting for you, ring 61212."

"Very well," said Stringer and, feeling like an outclassed boxer who has just heard the bell signalling another round of punishment, he put the phone down.

When the train pulled into Forebridge at four-thirty-five, he hurried past other passengers who had alighted and, waving his season ticket impatiently, squeezed through the barrier. Anders was there and opened the rear passenger door of the plain grey saloon as soon as he spotted him.

After it had been explained to him, a calm settled over Stringer. He seemed to be floating, unreal and looking down on himself. It was going to be difficult. They would have to move and, unless he could do something about it, it would be devastating for her.

"I don't think I was particularly helpful," he said to Anders. "I'm sorry about that now."

"Perhaps the worst part is over."

"Is it? She'll have to give evidence, won't she?"

"I'm afraid she will, unless he pleads guilty, and I can't see that happening."

When Anders and the policewoman had gone, Stringer went upstairs. She was in a deep, sedated sleep, with her face against the pillow and her mouth partly open. Streaks ran down her cheek where tears had disturbed her make-up and she looked ten years older. For some time he sat by the bed, his mind gradually soaking up the implications. A murderer and a filthy violator of children . . . and her! How would it affect her— knowing that there had been the most intimate bodily contact between them?

He went downstairs and found himself some cold ham and a few tomatoes in the kitchen. Then he watched television with the sound turned down, going upstairs at intervals to see how she was. It was nearly seven before she stirred and for several minutes she moved about restlessly. Then she sat up suddenly.

"It's all right, Mavis. I know all about it," he said quietly. "They sent for me."

She buried her head again.

"Don't blame yourself. It wasn't all your fault. Those... those children, I can't bear thinking about it. Look at it another way. If it weren't for you, he might still be at it. Think of all the children you might have saved."

"I'm no good. Why don't you leave me?"

"Can I get you anything? I don't suppose you've had much to eat all day."

"I don't want anything."

"Have some warm milk with some brandy. Mavis! Some warm milk and brandy?"

She nodded against the pillow. "I'll try."

Earlier that day Myall had been in trouble with his wife, a woman of volatile, Italian stock who often rushed in first and reasoned afterwards. Not that she hadn't cause sometimes to question her husband's activities the wrong side of the bed-clothes.

She had rung the garage and, getting no answer, had called in while she was out shopping. The place was locked up and Myall nowhere to be seen. Her mind jumped past suspicion to near certainty and she returned home, her anger brewing steadily until Myall arrived.

"So! You've been at it again, have you?"

"What're you talking about?"

"You know what I'm talking about. You and that Elsie Winch! Same as before, isn't it?"

"Don't be bloody daft!"

"All right. Where were you this morning? Not at the garage. I went there."

"Christ, woman! I could have been anywhere. Why there?"

"Because you've been there before, that's why. And because she lives just up the road."

"Here! You didn't go there, creating?"

"No, I didn't. I've got more pride. So you admit it now?"

"No, I bloody well don't. If you want to know, I was at the police station."

"It's the police station now? What for?"

"I can't tell you."

"Of course you can't. But I bet Elsie Winch could."

"Look here ! I was at the police station, I tell you."

Her anger mounted and she looked round for something to throw at him.

"All right. They made me go there. It was about this Stringer woman who's mixed up with Mellish."

She frowned. "Stringer woman?"

"You haven't heard that. It was about Mellish. They know he murdered those kids but they wanted my help to prove it. See?"

"Are you telling the truth?"

"Go and ask 'em but don't say you know what it was about."

So by the evening the name had got out. In the Forresters rumour, with a basis of fact and a few half truths, had deviated and expanded to ridiculous proportions.

"Dame by the name of Stringer. Bought a Renault."

"Been covering up for him, she has. Probably in on it all the time. Remember that other one?"

"Why isn't she inside then?"

"Maybe they're waiting, see. Haven't got enough on her to prove it, see. Not enough to *know*, they've got to prove it, see. I'd make her talk, the sodding cow, I would."

This was a small group, vociferous and ready as usual to exploit a moral principle as an excuse for violence. Reasonable types detached themselves or were shouted down, and the noisy ones gravitated to a corner and engaged in low, urgent whispers.

"I'm game."

"Why not?"

"Don't know her address."

"Look in the phone book and go to all of 'em."

"We can get five in your car, Sid. What about it?"

"If you like. OK, go in mine."

George Stringer listened to the ten o'clock news and then he undressed and put on his pyjamas. Quietly he went into the bedroom they had previously shared and she moved her head.

"Do you want another tablet to make you sleep?"

"No. I don't want to keep taking them."

"I'll come back in here, shall I?"

She began to cry again. "If you don't mind sleeping . . . with someone like me?"

"Don't be silly, dear. Things are different now."

He heard the first sounds of a disturbance as he climbed between the sheets: a car drawing up outside, doors banging and loud, coarse voices. He was about to turn out the bedside lamp when he sat up again. It sounded like the latch of the front gate and mumbling voices below the window. And then, louder—"That's a Renault! This *is* her house!" There were shouts of general agreement and a coarse laugh. Some kicked the front door.

She sat up. "George! What was that?"

Glass tinkled at the side and someone yelled: "That's it. Smash her bloody car for a start!"

He went to the open window and looked out. They seemed to be everywhere. "What are you doing there?" he said, trying to sound stern, but his voice, as always, lacked authority.

They looked up and one of them said: "It's her old man, I expect."

"Where is she? Where's the female bloody preying mantis? Send out the witch or we're coming in."

He rushed to the bedside phone and dialled frantically. As the operator's voice sounded, a large stone crashed through the window and glass flew across the room. Then there was

148

another and another, and from downstairs the sound of more crashing glass. He managed to get his message over.

"Go in the back room and lock the door," he said to her, and he went to a fitted cupboard.

"What are you going to do?"

He pulled out a cricket bat.

"You're not going down there!"

"I've got to, or they'll be in before the police arrive."

"But, George . . ."

Another stone found its mark and the glass sprayed round her feet. "Come on," he said, "into the back room and lock the door."

He didn't put on the lights and when he flung open the front door a man who was about to kick it nearly fell inside. Stringer hit him and he staggered back, clutching his head. There was an angry roar and another, larger figure appeared. Stringer wielded his bat again but this time it struck an upraised arm. A hard toe caught him on the knee cap but he found room to swing the bat once more. Then a large, rock-like object cannoned off the wall on to his face and he collapsed to the ground.

He was trying to get up again but they were retreating, running to their car. A police siren, and then another, became louder. He felt her arm under his head and heard her say: "George! Oh, George! You're bleeding."

CHAPTER 15

While five men were appearing before the magistrates on charges arising from the incident at the Stringers' home the previous evening, Jordan and Anders were again interviewing Mellish.

Jordan gave the caution and then said: "I want you to listen carefully to what I have to tell you. Mrs. Stringer has now made a statement to the effect that she has been having an affair with you and that between three o'clock and four o'clock on the following dates of this year you drove her husband's car while she was at the hairdresser's near Coolidge: Friday, 9th January, Friday, 23rd February and Friday, 6th April, and also between three o'clock and four o'clock on Tuesday, 5th June, while she was at her dressmaker's in Forebridge. What have you say to that?"

If Mellish was disturbed by this, he didn't show it. "The only part which is true is that I was having it off with her. I've never driven her husband's car."

Jordan and Anders noted his reply and then Jordan said: "Later today you will be charged with the murder of three children at Coolidge on the dates mentioned."

He stood up and, when it became clear that Mellish would say nothing more, he shut his notebook, nodded at Anders and they both left the room.

After they had gone, Mellish still sat apparently unmoved, but his mind was working overtime adjusting to this new development.

Lewis Wynn wasn't able to attend when Mellish was charged but he called in shortly afterwards. He dropped his case on the table and sat down.

"Now it's murder, or rather murders, and they've taken the unusual step of including all of them."

"They can't do that, can they?"

"Oh yes, they can. Whether or not the judge allows it is another thing, and naturally we'll lodge a strong protest."

"What are the chances?"

Wynn surveyed Mellish with a bleak, detached expression. "Normally, I don't think it would be allowed, but this isn't a usual case. Too much depends on it. One murder on its own wouldn't hold up, but put them together and they've got something. If Mrs. Stringer is telling the truth, we could be in trouble. Coincidences can only be stretched so far."

"She's not telling the truth."

"I asked you if you'd been seeing her and you said you hadn't. And *I'm* supposed to be defending you!"

"I'll admit one thing and that's all there is to it. You remember the day this other kid disappeared, the local one, Angela somebody-or-other?"

"Yes?"

"She'd been on at me and I suppose I felt like it. I was with her all the afternoon and most of the evening, in her car. I never left her. We were shagging each other in the car in the quarry when her old man and somebody else caught us. They didn't do anything then and I'm bloody sure neither of them saw much of me. Anyway, the next day I was worried, not wanting to break up a marriage and all that, so I rang her. That's when I agreed to help her buy her own car. She said

151

she didn't want to use his after that, but her husband wasn't saying anything."

"So you didn't meet her in the High Street?"

"Oh yes, I did. That was the day before we were caught in the quarry."

"Are you trying to tell me she hadn't seen you since you did the job on her bathroom?"

"That's right. But there's something else. Before I'd finished that job I'd had it with her and Christ, did she like it!"

"I see. So you met by chance and she suggested meeting again?"

"She didn't suggest it. She almost begged me."

"This is definite, is it? You were together all the time on the day this other child, the one who hasn't been found yet, disappeared?"

"That's right."

"How can you prove that?"

"If she keeps on lying, I don't know. We went to a tea shop in Freeling at about four. They might remember."

"Why is she lying?"

Mellish assumed an expression of genuine perplexity. "I don't know. Unless she's bitter about it. I went out with her a couple of times after and then decided I'd had enough, so I told her."

"What did she say?"

"Went into hysterics. I just got out of the car and walked home. She was too much for me."

"And that was the last you saw of her?"

"It was."

"When was that?"

"I don't remember. About a couple of days before they nicked me."

"Are you telling the truth this time?"

"Of course I am. What have I got to lose now? I'd be a fool."

"You didn't kill those children?"

"No, I didn't. Whoever killed this other kid probably did."

"I'll do what I can. I've spoken to Mr. Hector Browne and I think he will defend you. We'll have to accept the committal proceedings and not make too much fuss."

"This tea shop in Freeling," said Mellish. "It's called the Copper Kettle. A dark, fat woman served us. You ask there; they'll prove it."

At ten-thirty on the 14th August the committal proceedings began. Mr. Jeffrey Mays, a slight, dapper man with an avuncular manner, outlined the case for the Director of Public Prosecutions.

"Your Worship, this case hinges on the identity of the murderer of the three children mentioned in the charge. There is no direct evidence but the prosecution will establish beyond reasonable doubt that the accused is the person responsible. The police have been looking for a man with evil and abnormal tendencies. One was of getting into his car a little girl he did not know by using some persuasive pretext. The second was of taking the child into some remote part and then sexually assaulting and suffocating her.

"By the presentation of evidence, showing photographs found in the accused's room, and by identification of the accused as the man who abducted Peggy Finney, these abnormalities, we will prove, are possessed by the accused. In addition, to strengthen the charge, it will be shown that the accused lied repeatedly to cover his movements at the material times and that, in contradiction of his statement, evidence will be given to prove that on each single occasion when the murders were committed he was in sole possession of a car similar to that used by the murderer and the man abducting Peggy Finney."

Written evidence was accepted from all the witnesses except Peggy Finney and the coloured boy, Roddy Temple, who were both too young to make depositions.

The court was cleared before Peggy Finney, looking pathetically small and vulnerable, was shown into the witness box. Mr. Mays smiled at her, the clerk smiled at her and the magistrates smiled at her. Mellish stared at her.

"I believe your name is Peggy Finney?"

"Yes, Peggy Finney."

"And you live at 25 East Street, Forebridge?"

"Yes."

"How old are you, Peggy?"

"Seven, nearly eight."

"You're nearly eight, eh? You understand what telling the truth means?"

She nodded and then said: "Yes."

"Do you remember the 5th June?"

She nodded again.

"Why do you?"

"It was my mum's birthday."

"Is there some other reason?"

Another nod.

"What was that reason?"

"A man took me in his car."

"How did you come to be in his car?"

She explained falteringly but satisfactorily.

"You are quite sure he said 'Selly Park' and not 'Sethley Park'?"

She nodded.

"You are quite sure?"

"Yes."

"Now, look round the court. Can you see the man who took you in his car and to the common?"

The silence was intense as her eyes wandered over them. Then she pointed at Mellish. "That's him."

"The man between the two men in uniform?"

"Yes."

"Thank you, Peggy."

Roddy Temple told what he knew, but when asked if he could point out the man, he looked at Mellish, hesitated and then said defiantly: "I don't know. I'm not sure."

After the proceedings were over, the crowd hung about outside for some time and one of the last to leave was Joe Murray. He had spoken to no one, but before the court had been cleared he had seen him—the back of his head and side of his face when he turned—and he was satisfied that he would know him again.

Although the hollow, sickening ache was constantly with them, a degree of normality had crept back into the lives of Joyce and Joe Murray.

He again made the journey to town each day, catching later trains to avoid embarrassing his former travelling companions, and in his office he worked as efficiently as before but with a detached dedication.

To his wife he showed if anything greater consideration, but it was studied and automatic, and unintentionally lacking in warmth. She had turned more to him again, feeling strongly the desire to be needed. But there was something about him she couldn't define, and it worried her. At odd times, when apparently he was off his guard, he would retreat inside himself and would hear nothing and see nothing. She could pass in front of him and he wouldn't know it. Neither did he always reply if she spoke to him. Occasionally when he was like this there appeared in his unseeing eyes an expression which sent a chill of fear running through her. It was as if a blind had been drawn back momentarily, giving a glimpse of some dreadful, destructive energy waiting there and biding its time. "Joe!" she would say. "Are you all right?" and gradually his eyes would soften and he would blink once or twice. "Yes, dear, you were saying?"

She knew he was going to the court for the committal proceedings and she was uneasy about it.

"Why? It won't bring her back and thinking about that side of it only makes matters worse," she said. "I know I went to pieces at first and things will never be the same, but it doesn't help."

"I've got to go. There's a reason."

"What reason?"

"I'm sorry. Don't keep on. There is a reason, that's all."

When he came back after the first day, she looked at him anxiously.

"I saw him," he said.

Although he had not advertised the fact, Anders was now convinced that Mellish had had nothing to do with the disappearance of Angela Murray, and the question of her possible fate had to be reconsidered. The intensive search had been called off, for the further it spread from the centre the more impossible it became, but a small task force was left to travel quickly to any likely place and her description and photograph were kept prominently in public view.

There was one another thing which puzzled him: the wig and raincoat in Mellish's possession when he had been arrested. Mellish had refused any explanation but it could be reasonably assumed that he had intended to use them for some nefarious purpose. With this in mind, Anders drew up a list of relative information:

1. Established that Mellish was on his way to meet Mrs. Stringer.
2. He had broken his usual pattern by walking instead of using his car. Why was this? (It would have taken him half an hour to get to their rendezvous.)
3. Where were they going? Mrs. Stringer has said that she usually left it to him and it was rarely the same place twice. Also it was usually some distance from Forebridge.
4. What possible purpose could the wig be for? To put on someone—himself presumably.
5. Why should he want to put it on? Not to improve his appearance for sure! The only other possible reason was for disguise.
6. The raincoat tended to confirm this. The two together would alter his appearance considerably.
7. When did he intend to put on the disguise? Not to meet Mrs. Stringer or while he was with her surely?

And not for some purpose on the way to meet her, there wasn't time.

8. Why would he need a disguise? To confuse identity if seen committing a crime?
9. What sort of crime? Housebreaking? Robbery? Not very likely. It was out of character and there was no need for it.
10. What was in character? The answer rushed at the question—murder! A disguise to avoid recognition as he made his way from the scene back home!

Anders blew through his lips as the distinct possibility occurred to him.

11. If so, who had he intended to murder? The logical answer was: the person he was going to meet. And he had a strong motive. She was the only person who could put the finger on him. Without her evidence there would be no case as far as the murders were concerned.

He polished up the notes he had made, had them typed and put them on the file.

He then turned his attention again to Angela Murray. Whatever happened to Mellish, there could be no satisfactory conclusion until her disappearance had been cleared up. It was possible that they would still find her, but not surely in the locality or the surrounding district. The search had been thorough and efficient and reflected great credit on everyone concerned. One day perhaps, maybe years ahead, small decaying bones would be found in some faraway, remote spot and the issue raised again.

Now Mellish had been ruled out, could her disappearance be linked with another more personal motive? He reflected on Jordan's broad remarks about Mrs. Murray and he decided that an entirely new approach to the problem was called for.

The Murder Headquarters at Coolidge and at Forebridge

were being closed down and Anders had arranged for essential material to be moved to a room in Forebridge police station which was now adequate for the purpose.

On the afternoon of the second day after Anders had moved to the police station, there appeared one of those bolts from the blue which, while throwing disorder into previous calculations and theories, also provide new life in a different direction.

He had a visitor: a healthy-looking, well-dressed man of about forty by the name of Robert Pavey. Mr. Pavey lived in Leicester but he frequently visited his mother in Forebridge. He had recently returned from a business trip to Canada and this was the first time he had seen his mother since he left, which was on the afternoon Angela Murray had disappeared. Having seen the posters and pictures of Angela, and having spoken to his mother, he had remembered something which he felt might be of some help.

On the day concerned, he had left his mother just after three o'clock to drive to Heathrow. His route took him along Baddow Road and he remembered one incident which occurred about two hundred yards past the school. He had been following a car for several minutes when rather suddenly it slowed down and stopped as it was passing several parked vehicles on the nearside. As there was no room to overtake, he had been forced to stop. The driver of the car in front, a woman, had wound down her window and called to a small girl who was walking along the footpath in the same direction. After a short conversation, the girl got into the car and it drove off, turning down the next road on the right. The girl was dressed in the same school uniform as that shown in the posters and, from the brief sight he had of her, of similar appearance. The woman had dark hair. He had seen only the back of her head and her profile, and he had the impression that she was on the thin side. The car, to the best of his recollections, was a cream or white saloon, but nearer than that he couldn't go.

Anders made a mental note to enquire who had called at the mother's house and why they hadn't found out that she'd had a male visitor on that day and, making an excuse, he left Mr. Pavey in the office, shut the door and sought out the desk sergeant.

"The man who's called to see me, does anybody know if he's got a car outside and what it is?"

The sergeant didn't know but a constable near the window said: "I saw him get out, sir. It's a red Volvo, parked outside."

"Good. Without making it obvious, get the number and all the details and have a look inside."

Anders went back to Pavey, apologized for leaving him and then plied him with more questions. In the end he was favourably impressed with him but, nevertheless, when Pavey had gone he telephoned a contact at Leicester and asked him to find out all he could about him.

Then, after pondering on this new development, he decided. He sent for Detective-Sergeant Hudson, Detective-Constable Hockett and Detective Woman Constable Forbes and explained what he wanted from them.

"It's a delicate matter and we don't know where it might lead. On no account are the Murrays to find out that you are making these enquiries. Any information from them must be of a casual nature. You are to work as a team, reporting to me at least once a week but as often as you feel is necessary."

There were a few points to clear up and then they left. Although they had little to go on, they knew what was wanted, and Anders was satisfied that he had chosen well. It was rather ironic, he thought, that Hudson would never be an inspector because he couldn't pass the sergeant's exam. They both had exceptional qualities and were first-class thief-catchers. Yet they would often have men over them, telling them what to do—sometimes with a display of condescending arrogance— who wouldn't be able to hold a candle to them.

By the end of the first week some progress had been made but, owing to the restrictions imposed by discretion, not as much as they would have liked.

Joe Murray, they had found, had been born and brought up in Bournemouth. He had gone to a grammar school there and had later been articled to a local firm of accountants. His sporting activities were considerable and in the field of rugby football he had at one time been almost a national figure. He had a brother who was a doctor with a practice at Beaconsfield and a married sister who lived in Totnes. Both his parents were dead.

Joyce Murray, née Christian, was born in Wokingham. And that was as far as they had got.

The next week more information was added. Mrs. Murray's parents had parted when she was three and her father had gone to live in America where he had re-married. She hadn't seen him since. She and her sister, Gladys, who was two years older, had been brought up by their mother with considerable help from the grandparents. She had been educated at a private school in Reading. Gerald Christian, her grandfather, had been a rugby enthusiast and a partner in the firm of accountants where Murray now worked. It was through him that the two had met.

By the third week there was further information of this nature but nothing which appeared to have any significance.

However, towards the end of the fourth week something emerged which caused Anders to hesitate and search a bit deeper. Murray had first courted Gladys Christian and would probably have married her. But when he met Joyce Christian, who returned from an extended holiday abroad, there had been a strong mutual attraction.

Anders gave instructions to concentrate attention on Gladys Christian, and by the middle of the following week learned that she was still unmarried and lived alone in a secluded cottage near Basingstoke where the usual enquiries had been made soon after the girl's disappearance. The grandparents and her mother were now dead.

CHAPTER 16

On the 8th October, Mellish's trial at the Crown Court began.

Dressed in a brown suit, fawn shirt and a wide maroon tie, he was flanked by two prison officers but he was not hand-cuffed. As he appeared, an air of tense excitement and sup-pressed hostility ran through the crowded court. There was not a friendly face, not one person who would willingly have lifted a finger to help him. Apart from his counsel he was on his own. Curious glances were cast at him, at the handsome face, the unwavering stare from the dark eyes and the im-passive expression.

Mr. Justice Redman took his seat and immediately, even before the jury had been selected, Mr. Hector Browne, who led for the defence, raised an objection which, if upheld, would undoubtedly have had a most profound effect on the course of the trial.

He was a long, gangling man with heavy features and a petulant, slightly bored expression on his face most of the time, which was misleading. He spoke in a deep voice, eco-nomically and, except when he was paying due deference to the judge, as if it would be quite absurd for anybody to disagree with him. He was renowned for finding loopholes in the most cast-iron cases and, if this didn't always win the day for him, it considerably narrowed the margin of defeat.

Making a strong application to have the abduction charge and the murder charges tried separately, he said: "It will be impossible for my client to have a fair trial on the murder charges if they are heard together in conjunction with the abduction charge. Any jury will automatically be biased."

For over an hour he consulted law books and cited previous decisions. There were arguments and counter-arguments. At the end the judge gave his ruling.

"It is true that hearing these cases together will be gravely prejudicial to the accused, but equally it is important that justice should be done. While it is essential to avoid anything which might in any way help to convict an innocent man, it is also important to make sure that a guilty person in such a case as this is not acquitted. The consequences could be dreadful, and I think there is here a sufficient pattern established to justify that the present arrangements should stand."

The first round had gone to the Crown.

The twelve jurors were sworn in, including four women, and much to the surprise of the prosecution there were no objections from the defence.

In a firm voice Mellish pleaded not guilty to all the charges.

Mr. Cyril Baker led for the Crown and it would have been difficult to have found a greater contrast between two counsels. He was much shorter than Mr. Browne and stockier, and even in repose his face seemed to mirror an alert interest in anything and everything.

It took him nearly two hours to outline the case for the prosecution and he finished by saying: "This is an unusual case because it relies almost entirely on circumstantial evidence. Scientific evidence is confined to a hair similar to that of one of the murder victims which was found in the car alleged to have been used by the accused, and samples of soil found in the car which is of similar composition to that found near one of the victims. However, when there is an abundance of circumstantial evidence it can be the strongest there is, and I submit that the evidence you will hear will prove that the accused was not only in a position to commit these crimes but that he was also without a shadow of a doubt the man who did."

Evidence was then given by police officers who had found the bodies of the victims and had photographed them, and from the pathologist who had examined them. The defense raised no questions and the court was adjourned until the following day.

In the evening, Anders heard from Hudson. They had booked in at a hotel in Basingstoke as they weren't entirely satisfied with Gladys Christian. Policewoman Forbes, posing as a consumer survey investigator, had called at the house and had come away with the impression that the woman was decidedly eccentric and somewhat evasive. The cottage was larger than they had expected and there were signs that Miss Christian was comfortably off but not over-bothered about cleanliness. The garden was surrounded by a high quick hedge and was just about tidy enough to be respectable. The nearest neighbour was a farmer who lived across the fields half a mile away. Several dogs had barked from the back of the house. At the side was a fairly modern garage but so far no vehicle had been seen.

Murray had been present during the first day of the trial and the resolve to kill Mellish, once he was sure he was guilty, had grown rather than diminished until it had become something in the nature of a sacred duty. Others in similar circumstances had vowed what they would do if they were given the chance, but time had dimmed the spirit of revenge. In Murray's case, to say that revenge was the motive was to oversimplify it. It was as if he owed it to her, his daughter, and to the other parents who had suffered and would continue to suffer for the rest of their lives.

And again Murray was different from most men. He didn't wait for chances, he made them. He had the intelligence and physical courage necessary, and in addition he had a fertile brain which previously had been used only for commendable purposes. He could have been a valuable secret agent, an adventurous and successful criminal. The potential had always been there waiting for a strong enough reason.

He wanted to hear the evidence but he also had things to do and so, before the court adjourned, he left to reconnoitre the area adjacent to the court buildings.

It didn't take him long to find out how and where the prisoners were escorted to and from prison. Behind the court was a yard surrounded by a wall, with heavy gates opening on to a quiet side road. The wall was a good eight feet high but, when no one was looking, he pulled himself up to the top of one of the gates and saw a blue prison van standing there.

Then he discovered the derelict churchyard and had almost walked past it before its possibilities came to him. Casually he lit a cigarette, waited for a suitable opportunity and made for the entrance. The broken gate creaked on its hinges as he pushed through and it creaked again as he shut it behind him.

A wind had sprung up and the dry, autumn leaves scurried over the hard ground, gathering against patches of scrub and in the dusty corners of the building. It was a depressing, forbidding structure made of unrelieved dark red brick and grey slates. Some of the long, gloomy windows had been broken and weeds were everywhere.

He passed over the uneven path at the side until he came to several old trees as neglected and forgotten-looking as the church itself. Suckers from them poked through the long grass. Behind the trees was the stone wall with broken glass firmly embedded along the top. He was completely hidden from view but he looked around for a while to make sure that he was alone and waited in case some inquisitive person had seen him enter and had decided to investigate.

Then he pulled himself on to the branch of a tree and, steadying himself against the trunk, stood on it. He could now see over the wall to the yard beyond. To the left was the rear of the court buildings, an expanse of grey and yellow brick with no windows. There was a wide, grey-painted door with stone steps leading to the yard. The van was still there.

He decided to wait.

He was beginning to feel the effect of his cramped position when the door opened and Mellish, handcuffed, came out with two prison officers and a driver. Murray reckoned that they were no more than fifteen feet from the wall. They trooped into the van and an elderly man opened the gates. Then they drove off.

Murray lowered himself from the branch and stood there thoughtfully for a few moments before he began to search in the long grass. In one corner he came across a few decaying boards from what had once been a small hut. He inspected them, put several of them aside and then he dusted himself down with his hands and went back to his car.

For some time he sat thinking. He needed a gun but, without drawing attention to himself, it would be extremely difficult to get one. He certainly couldn't do it legally and, in any case, time was against him. He needed one *now*—desperately. Somehow he would have to take that extra risk . . . somehow!

Then suddenly he remembered! The crossbow! Years ago he had nearly got rid of it. He had acquired it before he was married when he had become interested in old weapons. The other stuff had gone long ago but for some reason he had kept that. Joyce had never liked it, hadn't wanted it in the house, and it had been stowed away in the loft and forgotten. It was unlikely that anyone other than Joyce would know that he had it. It was a most lethal weapon and he could see no reason why it shouldn't still work effectively. At one time he had amused himself at target practice with it and had become remarkably proficient.

The more he thought about it, the more he inclined in its favour. True, a bolt from a crossbow would be a better lead for the police than a bullet, but it was a slim chance that they would trace it back to him—suspect what they liked!

When he got home Bill Surridge, his next-door neighbour, was pottering about in his front garden and Murray reversed past the building line and then went in the back way to avoid him.

He liked Surridge but he found that meeting friends or acquaintances could now be strained and awkward. After their first expressions of sympathy, what could they say? They couldn't keep it up for ever and pleasantries or everyday topics seemed crudely out of place.

And other people he had to brush shoulders with every day in trains and in the streets—they knew nothing of him or he of them, but their occasional light-hearted comments or laughter grated and sometimes, when he couldn't get away from them, he felt a strong impulse to shout them down and slap their grinning, fool faces. It was different with children. Their laughter hurt but it didn't offend.

Although he was full of sympathy for her, he found it difficult to talk even to his wife. She had once been an attractive woman but there were now haggard lines on her face and a dullness in her eyes. The skin round her neck had become loose and creased, and angles were replacing the curves in her figure. Perhaps when this was done and the hue and cry had died down—for he had no intention of being caught—then maybe they could gradually put it all behind them and start again.

She didn't hear him come in and at first he wondered where she was. Then a strangled sob guided him to the hall and he saw her half way up the stairs, crouched in a twisted, ungainly position with her face buried in her arms. He went up to her and touched her on the shoulder. "Joyce!"

Suddenly she scrambled up as if she wanted to get away from him, sobbing as she went. Their bedroom door banged as he hurried after her, and when he went in she was lying face downwards on the bed.

Then he noticed the piece of paper screwed up in her hand. Gently he loosened her fingers and took it away. It was a note, cold and brief, in an obviously disguised handwriting. "If you can't look after children, you deserve to lose them." That was all.

He put it in his top pocket and held her hand. "Joyce! Joyce! You mustn't take any notice of that. You mustn't."

"It's true," she said jerkily and without looking at him. "If I'd gone to meet her, it wouldn't have happened. That's true, isn't it?"

He frowned, the pressures making him irritated. "The person who wrote that is mentally sick. Have I ever blamed you? Surely that's what matters?"

"You haven't said so but you might think it."

"I don't think it. I never have and I never will. God! Can't you see that this is only making matters worse for both of us? Can't you see that?"

She twisted herself to a kneeling position and remained there wiping her eyes before she sat on the edge of the bed. "Stay and talk to me!"

"Yes, of course." He sat beside her, putting his arm around her. But he felt completely inadequate. Unless he had something worth saying, he was a poor conversationalist at the best of times.

"I'll *try* and forget it," she said.

"That's it."

After a long pause she said: "Do you *have* to go there any more?"

"Yes, I do. I must see it through. When it's over, we'll try again, shall we?"

She nodded against his shoulder. Then she said: "I left a ham salad for you in the refrigerator. I don't want anything."

"Nor do I at the moment. I'll think about it later."

For nearly an hour he sat with her. Then he persuaded her to go to bed and when, at half past eight, he found her fast asleep, it made it that much easier for him.

Apart from a thin covering of dust, the crossbow was as good as when he had last seen it. He took it, with the two bolts, into his garage.

The garage was just over twenty feet long with a workbench

167

running across the back wall. Tools hung neatly on one side and a heavy vice, its blue-grey metal shining and free from rust, was secured to the bench.

He sorted through some timber stacked against the wall and selected two pieces of four-by-two which he clamped side by side in the vice. Then he opened a bin of red paint, stirred it with an old brush and placed a blob on each piece of timber.

He took the crossbow to the opposite end of the garage and, pulling on the lever, secured the bowstring in its notch. He laid the bolt in the groove at the top, took careful aim and pulled the trigger. There was a screaming twang and the sharp metal tip of the bolt embedded itself into the wood within a few inches of the target. He shot the second bolt and this time he was almost on target. He practised for over an hour before he was satisfied.

Then he joined together three sheets of brown paper with Sellotape and made an odd-looking but neat parcel of the crossbow, which he put into the boot of the car. He locked the boot, drove the car into the garage and went to bed.

The first witness the next day was Peggy Finney. With kindly but impartial prompting from the judge, she gave her evidence and then Mr. Browne rose to cross-examine. He smiled at the small girl and said: "Hallo, Peggy. "

She said: "Hallo."

"I'm sure what you have told us is true but you won't mind my asking you about some of it, will you?"

She shook her head and looked round the court.

"Now, Peggy, you've told us about the man who asked you to go in his car and that he said 'Selly Park' and not 'Sethley Park.' I believe a policewoman asked you about this first. Is that right?"

"Yes."

"She asked you what happened and you said: 'The man asked me to show him where Selly Park was.' You said 'Selly' because you are a local girl and that's how you say it, is that it?"

She nodded and said: "Yes."

"Did the policewoman say to you: 'Did he say Selly?'!"

"Yes."

"So, if she hadn't done that, you wouldn't have noticed that he didn't say 'Sethley'?"

She seemed a little confused. "I don't know."

Mr. Browne smiled again. "I'm only trying to be absolutely sure that a mistake hasn't been made. You wouldn't like that, would you?"

"No."

"Do you like watching television?"

"Yes."

"Have you seen on television where a man who has done something wrong has to go to a court like this or like the one you went to before?"

"Yes."

"When you saw this on television, the man who had done something wrong, did he have one or two other men in uniform next to him?"

"Sometimes."

"So—" another smile—"when you saw a man like that in the other court you thought it ought to be the man who was supposed to have taken you in the car?"

"Yes, I suppose so."

Mr. Browne said; "Thank you, Peggy," and sat down.

Mr. Baker got up as if to re-examine and then, thinking better of it, sat down again.

Then the boy Roddy Temple was called and received similar treatment, with similar results.

Both counsel knew the dangers of pressing children beyond a certain point but, as far as the defence was concerned, something had been achieved. The jury would already have got the message.

Mrs. Conway, dressed in a well-cut, plum-coloured jacket and skirt, took the oath and looked round as if she were prepared to take on the whole court single-handed. She gave her evidence in a clear, firm voice and in a manner which suggested that she would deal harshly with anyone who contradicted her.

Mr. Hector Brown got to his feet but he didn't seem in any hurry to begin. He glanced down at the table and, after shuffling through some papers, took off his wristwatch and put it down in front of him. Then, with his head on one side and looking somewhere over Mrs. Conway's left shoulder, he said: "When you first saw this man, what part of him did you see?"

"What part of him? His back, the back of his head and his back mostly."

"You didn't see his face?"

"Of course not, not at first."

"Then he let the girl go, turned and went to his car?"

"Yes. Yes, that's right."

"After a few brief remarks you hurried after the child?"

"Yes, after he tried to cover up by making out he had something to do with her."

"As far as you can remember, what did he say to you?"

"I've already told you."

"I should like to hear it again," said Browne and looked down at the table.

"He said what a trouble he'd had finding her, that she was always running off and that her mother was worried."

Browne waited a few moments and then lifted his head. "Was that all?"

"Yes. That was all he said."

"I see. And you were concerned about the child?"

"I suppose I was. I wasn't sure."

"So you hurried after her and didn't see the man again?"

"That's right."

"You speak clearly and deliberately, Mrs. Conway, which is more than can be said for many people. Did he speak any more slowly than you did just now?"

"I don't think so. No."

"Am I right in saying that the time you were looking at his face coincided with the time he was speaking to you?"

170

"Yes, more or less."

"How do you mean—more or less? Was it more or was it less?"

She tested Mr. Browne with a piercing glare. "He was speaking to me while I was looking at him."

"And as soon as he stopped speaking you went after the girl?"

"Yes."

"Do you know how long it took you to say what this man said?"

"I've no idea."

"I timed you, Mrs. Conway, and if you doubt it I am willing to make a recheck. It was eleven seconds—less than a fifth of a minute. Will you accept that?"

"I've no means of disproving it. You could be right."

"I am right. This means, does it not, that you had a view of the man's face for only eleven seconds? Eleven seconds, Mrs. Conway! And yet you claim to recognize him and to identify him definitely again."

Mrs. Conway took a deep breath. "There is no question of my claiming anything. I know what I know." She pointed at Mellish. "That is the man I saw."

"I suggest it would be more accurate to say that you *think* the accused is the man you saw?"

"I don't think, I know."

"After only eleven seconds?"

"I don't care how long it was."

"Of course, I was forgetting. He was also shown to you at the police station, wasn't he?"

"I saw him at the police station, yes."

"With only two men with him, both police officers, I believe?"

"There were two police officers with him."

"What else did you see?"

"I don't understand."

"Didn't one of the police officers assault the accused?"

Mrs. Conway frowned fiercely as she thought this over.

"Come now, Mrs. Conway. You were there. You saw what happened. Is it that you only want to say what you think you saw if it is favourable to the prosecution?"

"Nothing of the sort! I was wondering how you might twist what I say to make it favourable to you," she said, and Baker thought, she's not doing too badly but I hope she's not drawn into saying too much.

"Then tell us what happened," said Browne, "and let the court place its own interpretation on it."

"One of the police officers hit him when he started to get violent."

"In what way did he get violent?"

"He started to shout and throw his arms about."

"Did you see him actually attempt to strike anybody?"

"He would have done."

"Did you see him? Please answer the question."

"No."

"So you can't be sure if he would have done?"

"It looked as if he would have done but obviously I can't be sure."

"Thank you for that reluctant admission. Did you know that just before he was arrested his mother had a stroke and was taken to hospital?"

"No."

"And did you know that on the pretence of taking him to see his mother, he was guided to the spot where you could see him?"

"No, I didn't know that either."

"I don't suppose you did. But perhaps you can understand now why he seemed annoyed and threw his arms about." Mr. Browne continued quickly so that she couldn't answer and perhaps destroy an impression of mutual agreement on that score. "To go back to the point of identification, you knew the other men were police officers, so anybody else had to be the man they wanted identified, isn't that so?"

She struggled to find the snare. "I knew it wasn't any of the police officers."

"So the accused must have been the man they wanted you to identify?"

"Well, yes . . . if you put it like that."

"There's no other way to put it, and I want you to be absolutely honest with yourself. Did this fact influence you in your identification of the accused?"

"No. I would have picked him out anywhere."

"After having seen him previously for only eleven seconds? You can be sure of that? Was this man dressed in the same manner as the accused when you identified him?"

"No. I've already said he had on a blue shirt and blue trousers then."

"What did you recognize about him?"

"His face . . . and his eyes."

"You have heard of people so alike that their best friends found it difficult to tell them apart?"

"Yes."

"Isn't it possible then that the man you saw on the common and the accused are so alike that they could be mistaken for each other?"

"I don't think so."

"I'm not asking what you think. Please answer yes or no. Is it within the bounds of possibility?"

"Yes, I suppose it must be, but most unlikely."

Mr. Browne hesitated as if he were going to continue and then said: "Thank you," and sat down.

Mr. Baker, grudgingly admiring Mr. Browne's technique but not displeased with Mrs. Conway, got up to re-examine.

"Having answered very frankly and honestly the questions of my learned friend, are you still satisfied that the accused is the man you saw on the common and who had abducted Peggy Finney?"

"Yes, I am quite satisfied."

The court then adjourned for the afternoon.

When the court resumed, the two officers who had first called on Mellish with the questionnaire gave evidence, and the examination by the defence was brief and apparently inconsequential.

Another officer followed who told how he had subsequently examined the engine of Mellish's Mini and explained how he knew that the cylinder head had not been removed and the vehicle was available for inspection. No questions were put to him by the defence.

Miss Watkins told how she was in the tobacconist's when a man she recognized by photograph came in. He was dressed in a blue shirt and slacks.

"Could you be sure, absolutely sure, that this man and the accused are one and the same?" Browne asked.

"Not absolutely sure, but I think it was," she said and Mr. Baker was more than satisfied. She hadn't fallen into the trap of being unreasonably dogmatic.

Anders then went into the box and explained how he had first detained and then arrested Mellish, and read from his pocket book the questions put to him and the answers he had given before and after he was charged.

"When did you make these notes of the conversations you had with the accused?" asked Mr. Baker.

"Those before he was charged as soon as possible after the interview, and those after he was charged at the time, sir."

"I believe you searched him when he was arrested. What property did he have in his possession?"

Anders listed the property found on Mellish and the wig and raincoat were produced. He told how, on searching Mellish's room, they had come upon the obscene photographs. These were also produced and, as he finished, the balance of probability had again swung in the prosecution's favour.

Hector Browne approached the cross-examination cautiously. He was now facing a professional and a worthy opponent.

"Would you agree, Superintendent," he said, "that these dreadful murders have caused strong emotional feeling, particularly in the district where they occurred?"

"Yes, sir."

"And police officers, being human and many with children of their own, have shared this feeling?"

"I expect they have, sir."

"Would you also agree that strong emotional feelings can have a deleterious effect on judgment?"

"They *can* have."

"For instance, one of your officers, Chief Inspector Carver I believe, struck the accused a violent blow in the stomach which had such a crippling effect that he had to be assisted back to wherever you put him?"

"Are you asking me a question?" said Anders.

"You agree that it happened?"

"I agree that Chief Inspector Carver struck the accused but not necessarily in relation to the words 'for instance'."

"You don't think the Chief Inspector was prompted by animosity when he struck the blow?"

"That I couldn't say. Some form of restraint seemed necessary at the time."

"Am I to understand that you approve of what happened?"

"No. I regret that it did but, until I know what might have happened if Mr. Carver hadn't acted as he did, I'm not in a position to criticize."

"It wasn't much of an identification, was it? One man and two known police officers!"

"As the accused refused to submit to a normal parade, it was the best we could do."

"The best we could do! The best we could do! Isn't that synonymous with everything about this case? The best you could do! Isn't it a fact that because of the similarity to the wanted man and because other circumstances might indicate that Mellish could be the man, you have tried to make everything else fit?"

"No, sir."

"I suggest that it is. Let us turn to the question of the photographs you found. Would you agree that, in most newsagents and bookshops in our main towns, magazines with articles and photographs of a highly sensuous and erotic nature are on regular display and in constant demand?"

"Yes, I would agree with that."

"The people who buy these magazines, they come from all walks of life?"

"I would say so, yes."

"Would you agree that, because they find pleasure in them, they do not necessarily have homicidal tendencies?"

"Yes, I would agree—not necessarily."

"Occasionally you may convict a person of a sexual crime, who is in the habit of buying them, is that so?"

"Yes."

"But not often?"

"Not as far as I know, but . . ."

"Could you say that any of these people would not have committed the crime of which they were charged if they hadn't looked at the pictures in the magazines?"

"I can't say that, but . . ."

"Did you know that it has been held by some authorities that, far from being a bad influence, such photographs can provide a relief in some cases and so prevent the individual concerned from resorting to violence?"

"I did know that, but . . ."

"You did know? Then why . . ."

Mr. Baker rose to his feet and protested. "I must ask, my lord, that the witness be allowed to finish what he is saying."

The judge looked down at Mr. Browne with mild reproach. "Yes, I agree. This tendency to interrupt is getting rather tiresome."

"I'm sorry, my lord. I didn't want the witness to stray from the point."

"Indeed! A police superintendent? Is he likely to?"

Browne cleared his throat and looked across at Anders.

"I was going to say," said Anders, "that others of equal authority hold the opposite view."

Mr. Browne moved his lips as if he were tasting something

176

sour. "The fact is, is it not, that there is no actual proof that erotic photographs have any effect in this respect either way."

"There is no actual proof, sir."

"One last question, Superintendent. Has the accused all through steadfastly maintained his innocence?"

"Yes."

"Thank you."

Anders half expected Mr. Baker to re-examine but the QC remained seated.

The court was adjourned for the day.

When Anders got back to his office there was a message asking him to ring Hudson and giving a telephone number. He got through on the third attempt.

"If it's all right with you, sir, we'll stay on here another night and see what turns up tomorrow," said Hudson.

"You think there might be something?"

"I don't know what to think but I'm not satisfied—none of us are. She's got a car, light beige, almost cream—a funny colour. It's a Vauxhall 4/90, about two years old. I don't think she's cleaned it for a long time and she'd never pass a test now, that's for sure. We followed her and how she keeps out of trouble is a mystery. We've checked locally and there's no traffic file on her."

"Have you managed to check the tyre casts?"

"No. That's a point. She stopped outside a supermarket here and we had a look, but the tyres are practically new."

"You didn't find out who changed them, I suppose?"

"No. I didn't think it a good idea. For one thing, there's an even chance we're wasting our time and, for another, I doubt whether whoever changed them would be able to pick out the old ones now. What do you say?"

"If you're not satisfied, stay there until you are," said Anders.

* * *

As he had done on the previous day, Joe Murray left the court after it adjourned. From what he had heard so far he was almost certain now and he had to be prepared.

Within a few minutes he had reached the abandoned church and when he was reasonably sure he would be unobserved he went in. Again he waited quietly for a while and searched the area. Then he went to the boards he had put aside and picked up several of them. These he propped against the wall, and when he stood on the ledge they formed, the top of the wall came up to his chest. The position he chose was to one side, so that anybody appearing from the building would not be looking towards him, and where also some straying branches of a tree provided a reasonable screen.

This time he didn't have to wait so long and, when Mellish came out between two warders, he took a sight line on him and through him to a distant object which he fixed in his mind.

After the van had driven away he climbed down, dismantled his makeshift platform and hid the wood behind a tree.

That evening, just as dusk was falling, he called to his wife: "I'm going out for a while," and without waiting for a reply he went to his car and drove away.

The church was a dark silhouette against the night sky and he cruised past it several times before he decided to stop. Then he got out and lifted the boot and, with his head inside, waited for a convenient moment. Two people passed, talking animatedly, and then another who seemed in a hurry. As soon as there was a lull in the traffic flow, he took out the crossbow, shut the boot and walked unhurriedly through the church gate.

When he got to the end of the building, he moved slowly into the deeper shadows and waited, listening, for a while. There was always the chance of running into a courting couple in need of privacy or a tramp looking for temporary shelter.

Motor vehicles outside on the road roared past spasmodically. Footsteps, voices and occasionally laughter echoed suddenly and just as suddenly faded away. Somewhere a dog barked and from a plane there was a menacing hum which seemed to linger persistently. But, apart from an occasional stirring of grass in the wind, the courtyard was silent and still.

Nevertheless he looked into every corner before he stripped off the brown paper, folded it and placed it under several large stones. He found a rather inaccessible corner for the crossbow which he covered with grass and bracken. Then he returned home.

CHAPTER 17

There were still three witnesses for the prosecution: Dr. Bowman, a member of the Forensic Department, Chief Superintendent Jordan and Mavis Stringer, and in this order they were called to the stand.

Dr. Bowman explained the composition of hair and how the specimen found in the car was similar to that found on one of the victims. He had examined one of Mrs. Stringer's hairs and it certainly didn't come from her. He also explained the composition of the soil samples found in the car and how it compared with that to be found at one of the murder spots. In cross-examination he had to admit that he could not say categorically that the hair came from the dead child and that soil similar to that exhibited was spread over a fairly wide area.

When Jordan was called, he walked to the witness stand like an elderly guardsman and to Anders, who watched his grey, rugged face as he gave his evidence, he seemed to be making a supreme effort. He spoke more slowly and deliberately than usual and he made few references to his pocket book.

Mr. Browne eyed him shrewdly. "You are the officer in charge of the enquiries into the Coolidge murders?"

"Yes, sir."

"For how long have you been so engaged?"

"About nine months now."

"Nine months? Continuously."

"Yes, sir."

"Have you had much rest in that time?"

"Not very much."

"So I expect you have often been very tired?"

"That is true, sir."

"At what stage in your investigation did you consider you had sufficient evidence to charge Mr. Mellish with these crimes?"

Jordan remained silent for what seemed an over-long time and heads turned towards him. Then he said: "When I was satisfied that he had driven Mr. Stringer's car on each of the afternoons when the murders were committed."

"When *you* were satisfied?"

"I and the other officers involved."

"It must have been a great strain. Would you agree that it is possible for overtiredness to affect judgment?"

"It is possible but my judgment was not affected."

"Answer me this, then. If it is proved beyond doubt that the accused did not drive this car on even one of the material dates, would you still have enough evidence to charge him?"

Mr. Baker jumped to his feet to protest. "My lord, the question is surely out of order. Mr. Jordan is not here to give his opinion on hypothetical situations. The accused has been charged and it is for the court to decide when all the evidence has been heard."

The judge adjusted his spectacles and looked down at Mr. Browne. "The objection is upheld," he said.

"Very good, my lord. There are no further questions."

For the prosecution there was now only one witness left.

In his opening address, Mr. Baker had outlined the nature of the evidence to be given by the witnesses, including that of Mavis Stringer, and when at two-twenty-five precisely she was called to the stand, the slightly casual atmosphere which had inevitably developed changed abruptly. Even to the less sensational minds she was to be the star witness and, as far as the Press were concerned, a source of outstanding copy.

As she took the oath every eye was on her, curious and searching. Impressions were forming before she opened her mouth. Make-up had given her some colour and she was wearing a high-necked, navy dress which quietly suited her figure. She was extremely nervous and her voice faltered several times, but Mr. Baker's soothing manner gradually gave her confidence and by the time she had finished she was reasonably composed.

Anders had warned her. "You might get some rough treatment from the defence counsel. He won't spare your feelings. Try to remember that if you get upset this will suit him. Don't get drawn into arguments or rush into answering questions. You know the truth. Stick to it and avoid saying more than you need."

As Mr. Browne rose to his task, she tried to remember this and some defiance ran through her. The worst surely was out now, for the whole world to know! What did it matter?

Mr. Browne began quietly, almost considerately. "I should like your help on one point, Mrs. Stringer. Will you cast your mind back to the 4th June, a date which so far hasn't been mentioned. Has it any significance to you?"

"I . . . I don't know . . . quite what you mean?"

"Would that be the day when your husband first found out that you were being unfaithful to him?"

"Yes."

"Now I'm sure you can remember. How did you occupy your time on that day from say half past two until nine o'clock?"

"I spent it with Peter Mellish."

"The whole of the time?"

"Yes."

"What did you do together?"

Mr. Baker rose to his feet. "My lord, is this necessary? We

have already established the former relationship between the witness and the accused. Need we make it more painful for her?"

The judge raised a bushy eyebrow at Browne.

"My lord," said Browne, "my cross-examination of Mrs. Stringer is vital to my client. I have no wish to embarrass her unnecessarily but certain truths can only be arrived at if approached in the right direction, as you will see when I call the accused to the stand."

"Very well, you may proceed."

Mr. Browne looked across at Mrs. Stringer again. "I will repeat the question. What did you do together?"

"We went for a drive out in the country in the afternoon. We had tea in a shop in Freeling."

"How far is that from Forebridge, do you know?"

"About thirty miles."

"Can you give any idea of the time you got to the tea shop?"

"About half past three."

"And how long did you stay there?"

"Nearly an hour, I should think."

"So from half past two until nearly half past four you were either driving from Forebridge or in the tea shop?"

"Yes."

"Together all the time?"

"Yes."

"After you left the tea shop, what did you do?"

"We went for another drive."

"Is that all? Didn't you have sexual intercourse together?" She looked down and Mr. Baker half rose in his seat.

"Yes," she said.

"Where?"

"In a field."

"I see. What happened then?"

"We drove back."

"What time did you get back to Forebridge?"

"I don't know. It was after seven."

"Then what did you do?"

She looked down again. "He suggested we went to the quarry."

"He suggested? Didn't you suggest it, Mrs. Stringer? Didn't you say: 'I must have you once more before we go home'?"

She raised her head, glanced at Mellish and frowned. "No, I didn't."

As if to humour her, Browne quietly said: "I see," and consulted his file. "What time does your husband come home?"

"About seven."

"Did he know you wouldn't be there?"

"Yes."

"Did he know what you were doing and who you were with?"

"No."

"What did you tell him then?"

"I told him ... I told him I was going to see a woman friend."

"You lied to him?"

"Yes."

"That wasn't the first time, was it?"

"No," she said faintly.

There was a considerable pause while Mr. Browne let that sink in. Then once again his tone was almost placatory. "This was also the day, was it not, that Angela Murray, a nine-year-old girl, disappeared from Forebridge?"

"Yes, that's right."

"The child was last seen at a quarter past four. Would you agree that the accused could not have had anything to do with her disappearance?"

"Yes."

"It would have been quite impossible?"

"Yes."

Mr. Baker had been surprised that the question hadn't been put to Anders, but he thought that he now saw the reason. Anders, under re-examination, might well have given a satisfactory explanation why this could be immaterial. Mrs. Stringer was in no position to do so.

"When you were in the quarry, I believe your husband found you?"

"Yes."

"But he had no idea then, or until recently in fact, of the identity of the man with you?"

"Yes."

"Yes he had, or yes he hadn't?"

"He hadn't any idea."

"Following this, did Mr. Mellish say that he didn't like going in your husband's car now that your husband knew about it?"

"Yes, he did say that. It was..."

"And when he rang you, you asked him to help you buy a car of your own?"

"He offered."

Mr. Browne shrugged. "It makes no difference. Now, Mrs. Stringer, I believe the police came to see you several times?"

"Yes, they did."

"What did they ask you?"

"Who had used the car."

"They asked you who had used the car. And what did you tell them?"

"I told them... that I did, most of the time."

"Did they tell you why they wanted to know?"

"They said the car was similar to the one... you know... and that they were checking a lot of others as well."

"Did they ask you if anyone other than yourself or your husband had driven the car?"

"Yes."

"And what did you tell them?"

"That... nobody had."

"Was that the truth?"

"No."

"No?" Browne's voice rose in astonishment and his manner changed. "Do you mean to tell us that, knowing of these most horrible murders of little children, and knowing that the police were working night and day to find the person responsible, you lied to them over such an important matter?"

She wilted under the attack. "I didn't..."

"You didn't lie? You were telling the truth?"

"No, I didn't mean that. I thought..."

"Mrs. Stringer! You lied to your husband repeatedly. Now you are telling us that you lied to the police but you are not lying now. Answer me this. Why did you wait until now to tell the truth, if it *is* the truth?"

She hung her head and the court was silent. Then she said: "I came to my senses."

"Until the time of his arrest, you were still seeing the accused?"

"Yes."

"Let us consider your feelings towards the accused at the time. What did you think of him?"

"I...I liked him...very much."

"Liked him? Is that all?"

"I suppose I loved him. I thought..."

"Did you ever have reason to believe that you couldn't trust him?"

"I didn't think so."

"Answer the question. Did you ever have reason?"

"No."

"Did you consider him industrious, hard-working?"

"Yes, I thought he was."

"Considerate?"

"Yes, until I found..."

"You idolized him, didn't you?"

"I don't know about..."

"You don't know? Weren't you willing to give up everything and go away with him, live with him as man and wife? Isn't this what you planned to do?"

For a few moments she seemed stunned and then she said: "Yes."

"You were completely infatuated with him, would have done everything to be with him and then suddenly it was all going

186

to end. Is it not true, Mrs. Stringer, that two days before he was arrested the defendant saw you and said that he wanted to end the affair because he'd had second thoughts and didn't like breaking up a marriage?"

"No, that's not true!"

"The truth? What would you know about that? I am suggesting that it *is* true and that your infatuation for him changed into a lust for revenge—passion to hate?"

"No! No!"

There was a sudden interruption from the back of the court. George Stringer was on his feet. "Leave her alone, you bastard! Can't you see she's had enough." A police officer moved towards him. "You're twisting it. She's not lying." The gavel rapped the desk and Stringer was removed.

When the court had settled down again, Browne continued. "As I was saying, Mrs. Stringer, it seems inconceivable that even someone as infatuated as you were should shield a murderer. Isn't the true situation that, when your lover had abandoned you, you sought to embarrass him in this way as an act of revenge, so that even if nothing came of it people would be suspicious of the accused?"

"No! No! No! Oh, God, no!"

"What do you think has happened to Angela Murray?"

"I don't know."

"Do you still think Peter Mellish is capable of these murders?"

"I *don't* know." She almost collapsed, sobbing, and Mr. Browne sat down.

Then Mr. Baker was speaking to her again and the Welsh inflection and quiet timbre of his voice had a soothing effect on her. "Why didn't you tell the police that the accused had driven your husband's car?"

"Because I didn't want anybody to know who he was, who I was going with."

"I see. After they arrested Mr. Mellish, why didn't you tell them then?"

"Because then, I thought . . . I know about Angela Murray

187

and that couldn't have been him. So I thought he couldn't have done the others."

"Then later you had reason to change your mind?"

Browne got up to protest but she said: "Yes."

That concluded the case for the prosecution and, after a brief consultation, the judge decided to hear Mellish, the one witness for the defence, before adjourning for the day.

Mellish proved to be a good witness. The lies were most convincing. It all seemed so logical and, with the question of Angela Murray still in their minds, the balance of probability hovered again. The almost certain non-involvement of Mellish with the disappearance of Angela Murray was the strongest factor. Mellish explained away the lies he had told about the cylinder gasket of his car. He had never had a blue shirt or slacks and the girl in the shop must have seen someone like him.

Then Mr. Baker began to make things awkward for him.

Half-way through his cross-examination, Anders was summoned outside. "Urgent message for you, sir, on the phone," said the sergeant who came for him.

It was Hudson. "Marvellous news, sir! We've found her! Mrs. Murray's sister had her."

"Is she all right?"

"She's OK. A bit dirty."

Anders felt the tension drain away and immediately thought of Murray. All their efforts and sacrifices now seemed worthwhile. "Go on! Tell me about it."

"We took a chance and broke in while the woman was out. The kid was locked in a room upstairs. Apparently she was walking home from school when her aunt rolled up. She calls to see them about once or twice a year. But instead of taking her home, she drove down Ferry Lane. Something about her aunt's attitude alarmed the girl and, when the car had to stop because of a parked vehicle, she got out and ran away."

"And lost a shoe?"

"That's right. The woman drove after her, caught her and threatened all manner of things."

"Is she mad?"

"No doubt about it. No doubt also by her rambling remarks that she thinks the kid ought to be hers. Knowing the history, we can see why."

"Was the girl treated all right?"

"She wasn't ill-treated. She was fed and the woman tried to amuse her by playing games with her. Pathetic, really. The woman's inside now and the girl's at the hospital for a check-up."

"How on earth did she manage to keep her under cover for all this time?"

"You might well ask. Mind you, although she's gone mental in some respects, she's no fool. For instance we found a stack of empty milk bottles at the back of the house. Instead of increasing her order from her milkman she bought the extra from a shop where they didn't know her and she was fly enough not to give the empties to her regular milkman. The extra food she needed she also got from a shop where she wasn't known. Remember too that the place is pretty isolated."

"Didn't the girl try and escape?"

"Oh yes, several times. But her aunt seems to have thought of everything. She told the girl that if she behaved she'd go back to her parents one day, but if she didn't she'd never see them again."

"Sergeant," said Anders, "I could kiss you!"

"I'd rather kiss Policewoman Forbes, if you don't mind, sir."

Anders returned to the court and quietly slid into his seat at the side.

Mr. Baker, his voice and manner now far from soothing, was addressing Mellish who was still at the witness stand.

"Now, let us see what you have actually admitted. You have admitted having an affair with Mrs. Stringer, of having sexual intercourse with her in her car and other places right up to, or rather just preceding, the time of your arrest. You say that the last time you saw her you were smitten with a sudden twinge of conscience for her husband—whom you had never seen and for all you knew might have deserved her infidelity— and that you told her you weren't going to see her any more. You say she has been lying about the times when you drove her car while you waited for her, and that she was the prime instigator of the whole business. Is that right?"

"That is correct. I have already told you so."

"Yes. Yes. I am just getting it into perspective as it all seems so incredible. Then you admit that you lied to the police when they asked you what you had been doing and you had not in fact been changing the cylinder head gasket but had changed a wheel bearing?"

"Yes."

"And the reason you lied was that they had begun to irritate you?"

"That's right."

"Why did you tell them you had called at the tobacconist's?"

"I called in the morning."

"Not in the afternoon?"

"No."

"You lied again. Because you were irritated?"

"Yes."

"It doesn't take much persuasion to cause you to lie, does it? Knowing that the police might find out you had lied, wouldn't they be likely then to call back and cause you even more irritation?"

"I didn't think they would find out."

Mr. Baker gave a short, sarcastic laugh. "You didn't think they would find out many things. A man just like you, believed to be you by one of the witnesses, dressed in a blue shirt and slacks, did call at the tobacconist's early in the afternoon. Don't you think that is a remarkable coincidence?"

"It might be. It wasn't me though."

"Let us move forward to the evening of your arrest. Among the articles in your possession were the wig and the raincoat produced in evidence."

Mr. Browne stood up abruptly. "My lord, I have advised

my client not to answer questions on this, as it might be prejudicial to him in another and unrelated matter if it were to come to court."

The judge pondered on the submission. "You say that he was carrying these articles for some criminal purpose which has nothing to do with this case?"

"I do, my lord. Not unnaturally he has refused to tell me what this purpose was or where he was going."

"My lord," said Mr. Baker, "can we believe this? I should like to put my point to the witness, and whether he answers or not is up to him. But I don't expect to get the truth from him anyway."

"Very well," said the judge.

Mr. Baker turned again to Mellish. "You admit that you were carrying these articles?"

"Yes."

"We have heard from Mrs. Stringer that you were going to meet her that evening. If this is true, and I firmly believe her, it is strange that you should do so on foot and carrying a wig and a raincoat hidden in a parcel. But then we must remember that she was the only person who could give the damning evidence against you that you had driven her car on the days when these children were murdered. You knew that the police were making intensive enquiries and that you might become at least a suspect and that it would then be a matter of time only before they linked the two of you together. But if you got rid of Mrs. Stringer, they would have little to go on.

"I put it to you. Is it true that you set out that night to murder Mrs. Stringer and then return from some distant place wearing the wig and the raincoat so that you would not be recognized if seen in the vicinity where the murder was to take place? Is that not the truth?"

Mellish stared bleakly across the court. "No. It's not true."

Baker sat down and Browne slowly got to his feet. "Were you going to meet Mrs. Stringer that night?"

"No."

"Are you innocent of all the charges?"

"Yes, sir, absolutely."

"Thank you."

While Mellish was being escorted back to the dock, Anders had slipped his note to the clerk, who read it and passed it to the judge. For a few moments the judge looked down at the piece of paper and then he lifted his head.

"Mr. Baker. Mr. Browne. You may begin your final speeches tomorrow, but before the court adjourns I feel it is my duty to tell you of something which has come to my notice. The girl, Angela Murray, has been found alive and unharmed."

There was a ripple of whispered conversation which increased in volume as they all stood up while the judge was leaving the court. For most of them the last point of doubt had been removed.

Mellish was led away.

He walked along the stone floor of the corridor between the two prison officers. He knew that he had lost the day. Grudgingly he had to admit that his defence had done well and, until this last piece of news, there had been a reasonable chance of acquittal.

If the bloody girl had to be found at all, she had been found at least a day too soon! Now, unless he did something about it, the bleak prospect of gaol for twenty years or more stretched before him. But there was one thing in his favour which wouldn't have existed if things had gone against him in the ordinary way. As it stood, they wouldn't expect anything from him. The trial wasn't over, and he had been a model prisoner.

With such an eventuality in mind he had worked out exactly what he would do. Each evening when they had taken him back to prison, they had emerged into a yard where the van was waiting. There was a high wall surrounding the yard but the gates, which were opened by an elderly attendant who looked like a retired bluebottle, were not all that high: six feet at the most. And he had noticed, to the right, the top of an old church appearing over the wall. He had seen it and the broken windows as he stood at the top of the steps leading down into the yard. As soon as he descended, the wall hid it from view. But it was there, which meant there must also be a road in front of it.

If he acted promptly, and was lucky, he could be over the gate before they had recovered. And by the time they had the gate undone, he could be round the corner and in the church-yard before they knew where he had gone. He wouldn't stay in the churchyard though. He'd do what no one would ever expect of him: over the wall and back to the passage which ran from the yard. It was hardly likely that anyone would see him and he would stay there doggo. They would scour the neighbourhood but anywhere belonging to the court was the last place they'd look once they knew he had hit the road.

There was another advantage to it. There'd be no more than three of them and the old boy to start with. Two, in fact, because one would have to go back to sound the alarm.

There were two main obstacles. Could he deal adequately with the prison officers and would somebody outside obstruct him or see where he went? In the first case, he felt reasonably confident. When the bloody copper had hit him before, he hadn't expected it. His belly had been stretched and his stomach muscles relaxed. But this time *he* would take the initiative and he knew his own capabilities. Just a few minutes, that was all he needed.

Once outside, that would be different. He would have to make it to the corner quickly so they wouldn't know which way he had gone. Then, unless he wanted to attract attention, he would have to act normally, walk quickly maybe but not run. And he'd have to choose the right moment to enter the churchyard as long as he didn't waste time over it.

There were the handcuffs and he'd thought of a way round them. He had a large, clean handkerchief ready for the purpose and he would make sure one corner was sticking out of his pocket ready for a quick flick. This would cover his hands and wrists. What more natural than somebody walking along with a handkerchief at his nose?

Once he was safely over the wall and the hue and cry had died down, he knew where he was going—Warrens' Metal Shop. Years ago he had worked on a job for them there. It wasn't big enough for a night watchman but they had the tools. Christ, if he couldn't get the bloody handcuffs off, he didn't deserve to get away!

After that he would lie low again. He knew a few places. Change his appearance, his style, and then a ship somewhere! Escapes were made from the most unlikely places and people were always surprised. If you told them beforehand how it could be done, they wouldn't believe you. It was risky, of course it was, and he'd need some luck. But he had nothing to lose, absolutely nothing.

Lewis Wynn was waiting for him in one of the small ante-rooms at the end of the corridor. "We've done our best but now this girl's turned up..." He shook his head.

"It's not over yet."

"Frankly it's as good as. Your secrecy over the wig and coat hasn't helped. If only you'd cleared that point!"

"I'm not going to. But I want an appeal if I do go down. Don't forget that. Then I'll say what I had them for and prove I wasn't going to see her."

"If you can do that—prove you weren't going to see her—it will mean she was lying about it and you'll be clear. Why not now?"

"I've got my reasons."

Wynn shrugged resignedly and made for the door. "I'll see you tomorrow."

As the door opened, Mellish, for the benefit of the prison officer, called out: "If I go down, I want an appeal and then I'll tell them."

Not far away in one of the witnesses' rooms, Anders and Jordan were alone together. Now it was nearly over, Anders thought about Jordan again and looked down at him as he sat slumped in a chair. "You'll be able to take it easy after this for a bit. You must have a holiday."

Jordan stared ahead and a wistful smile hovered on his lips. "A holiday? Yes, Matt, I'll be taking a holiday." He glanced up. "If I tell you something, have I your word it'll go no further?"

"Of course."

"Not long before all this started, I was told I had no more than twelve months."

Anders declined to believe the implication. "You mean... They want you to retire?"

Jordan shook his head and smiled again. "They know nothing about it, otherwise I'd be out. Until I go sick, the police surgeon has no cause to come near me. Only my own doctor and the specialist and myself... and now you, know. I reckon I've got maybe six months left. They wanted to open me up and mess me about, but they said there was hardly any chance anyway and I wasn't having that. This way's best. Keep going and die in harness. But I'd have hated it if I'd gone before this case had been cleared up. I was dreading that happening. That's why I've told you, Matt. You've been a great comfort to me over the last few months and it's largely due to you that we've had the success we have."

Jordan's craggy face seemed to dominate Anders's view so that it was all he could see. He might have been watching him in close-up on television. "I don't know what to say. Hell! Are you sure?"

"You know I am. But no sympathy, please. It would spoil things. The job's been my life, although sometimes I've hated it."

Anders started to say something but Jordan interrupted and stood up. "I've told you. Now we won't mention it again."

Silently Anders studied him. Then he nodded and they both went out.

They handcuffed Mellish and led him from the cell. The drill was automatic. There was a prison officer in front and one behind, and the civilian driver went ahead. A uniformed attendant opened the door for them and the first lucky break occurred. The officer immediately in front of Mellish turned suddenly. "Sod it!" he said. "I've left nearly twenty fags behind. Won't be a minute," and he hurried back along the corridor.

To Mellish it seemed a remarkably good omen.

The elderly attendant appeared with a bunch of keys and without a word limped over towards his post by the gate. Mellish timed it perfectly. Pivoting suddenly, he crashed his knee between the legs of the officer who was behind him and a little to the side. Then, without pausing, he swung his manacled fists at the driver who, startled, had turned from opening the van. He was staggering sideways when Mellish helped him on his way to the ground with another savage blow, kicking him hard in the face as he fell.

The van had partly obscured the incident from the attendant at the gate but he knew something had happened and, as Mellish ran towards him, he advanced with slow determination. Mellish made as if to evade him, then, changing direction suddenly, he stopped, leaned back and thrust a vicious heel at the man's knee cap. The attendant rolled over, grimacing with pain, and Mellish stamped on his head as he ran forward. For a bonus, Mellish grabbed the keys and threw them high over the wall.

Just before he pulled himself over the gate, he glanced back. The first officer was still doubled up in pain and the driver was pushing himself off the ground, his face a mask of blood.

As Mellish dropped to the other side, he heard a shout and guessed it might be the third officer who had returned, but his immediate problem was the passers-by.

Again he was lucky. A man and a woman turned to look at him and then, perhaps because they hadn't seen him come over the gate or noticed the handcuffs, walked on again without further interest in him.

He ran lightly on his toes and by the time he had reached the corner he was holding the handkerchief to his face and strolling casually towards the church. He paused to blow his nose while two women went by and then he went through the gate.

Joe Murray had heard the first part of Mrs. Stringer's evidence but he had left the court before Mr. Browne began his cross-examination. There was no point in staying and he was not anxious to see and hear the humiliating indignity she was bound to suffer in public.

He was sure now! Mellish was guilty! Mellish—the evil predator who had selected Angela for his prey and had left her, like the others, out there somewhere!

Most of his waiting time he walked, returning to the court-house from time to time to make sure nothing had gone wrong and that they hadn't adjourned unexpectedly. There was, of course, the possibility of it continuing well into the late hours but he guessed that the case hadn't yet reached the stage when this was likely to happen.

When he thought there should be about an hour to go, he made his way to the derelict church building. He checked that the crossbow with its bolt was still there at the back and he pulled it clear. Then he sorted out the planks and leaned them as before against the wall to form his ledge to stand on.

After that it was a question of waiting patiently again and not once, alone with his thoughts the whole time, was he ever remotely deterred from his purpose.

Then it came, the sound of a bolt being pushed back and a key turning, and the movement he had practised twenty times before took no more than a second. By the time the leading prison officer appeared, he was aiming the bolt of the crossbow to the predetermined point which he knew Mellish would pass, and he was ready to make any adjustment necessary. The lever was back, his finger on the trigger. He held his breath to prevent the slightest movement of the crossbow.

But Mellish never reached the target area. Murray, astounded, watched the action and, pulling back the crossbow, released the bolt and let it fall to the ground. He would have difficulty in hitting a moving target and there was the danger of injuring one of the others.

For the few seconds it took, he watched Mellish's triumphant engagement with the prison officers, but when he saw him making for the gate he gave way to his first act of incaution. His perch was safe enough if he were careful, but carelessness made it precarious. Turning hurriedly, his foot slipped and his fourteen-stone weight plunged downwards on to his ankle as it twisted on a rut, and he rolled over in agony.

Mellish had moved quickly once alongside the church building. He had to get back over the wall before they thought of looking round there. At first, directing his gaze to the top of the wall, he looked over Murray who was trying to get to a position where he could stand on his good leg.

Then Mellish saw him and he didn't stop to wonder what he was doing there. All he knew was that this man had seen him and had to be killed if his scheme was to have any chance of success. He would have to kill him and hide him under something before he got over the wall.

Murray was equally startled to see Mellish but there was no time for reflection. A leather-clad foot hit him behind the ear, sending him sideways. Having this advantage over most men, Mellish would have found the rest easy, but Murray had mixed with the best. He knew what was to come and, although his head was still singing from the blow, he acted instinctively. He continued to roll over and Mellish's next kick found thin air. A large hand grasped his ankle in a vice-like grip. Now off balance, he was thrown on to the rough ground and Murray, ignoring the screaming pain in his ankle, crawled frantically towards him.

Mellish almost scrambled clear but again those iron fingers grabbed his ankle and, when he tried to draw back his leg to kick out, he realized the strength of his adversary. As Murray got another grip on him, Mellish chopped with his manacled hands, but for all the effect it had he might as well have been striking at a block of stone. He managed to turn unexpectedly and for a moment thought he had got away. Then an arm like a thick bar of steel encircled his throat, another arm clamped round the back of his neck and he felt them lock together.

Futilely he thrashed around but the pressure increased remorselessly. His eyes wanted to burst from their sockets and his tongue hung from his mouth as if it were trying to escape. Then he sagged, unable to offer further resistance, and in a few seconds it was over. Mellish was dead.

For how long he never knew, Murray lay stretched on the ground without realizing that his stranglehold was on a corpse.

Then slowly and painfully he managed to stand up. He looked down at Mellish, whose tongue was still hanging out and his eyes protruding, and he felt a grim sense of satisfaction.

Now it was done, his mind began gradually to function defensively and constructively. As far as anyone need know, he had committed no crime. He had been defending himself against an escaped murderer whom he had seen run into the churchyard. But there was the crossbow! He couldn't take it now. They'd see him with it and ask questions.

He limped over to where it lay and picked it up. Then he hid it again. He had thrown the planks back where he had found them by the time the searching police officers appeared. They stopped in their tracks. Staring at Mellish, one of them said: "Bloody hell!"

"He tried to kill me," said Murray calmly. "But I beat him to it."

They looked at him in awe and one of them shouted to someone at the back.

"I've injured my ankle," said Murray. "Will someone give me a hand?"

They took him to hospital where they treated his sprained ankle and swollen face, and when they had finished he was helped out to the police car.

He had edged backwards into the rear seat before he found there was somebody else already there. It was Anders. The driver walked away out of earshot and lit a cigarette.

"How do you feel now, Mr. Murray?"

"Not too bad. A bit battered."

"I'll get to the point. I could ask you some interesting questions but I'm not going to. But the Coroner's Officer will, and the Press will be buzzing round. Be careful what you say. I presume you haven't heard the news about your daughter?"

Murray's head jerked round and Anders didn't prolong the agony. "She has been found safe and unharmed. We've told your wife and we've been looking for you. Mr. Murray! Mr. Murray!"

Murray had slumped back in his seat with his head turned away. But Anders had seen the tears streaming down his face. He opened the window and called the driver.

About the time Murray was hobbling eagerly up his front path, Mrs. Mellish, in hospital and still partially paralysed, beckoned the nurse. "Ask my Pete to come and see me," she said. "I know he will. He's a good boy."

27 million Americans can't read a bedtime story to a child.

It's because 27 million adults in this country simply can't read.

Functional illiteracy has reached one out of five Americans. It robs them of even the simplest of human pleasures, like reading a fairy tale to a child.

You can change all this by joining the fight against illiteracy.

Call the Coalition for Literacy at toll-free **1-800-228-8813** and volunteer.

**Volunteer
Against Illiteracy.
The only degree you need
is a degree of caring.**

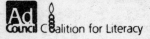

Ad Council Coalition for Literacy